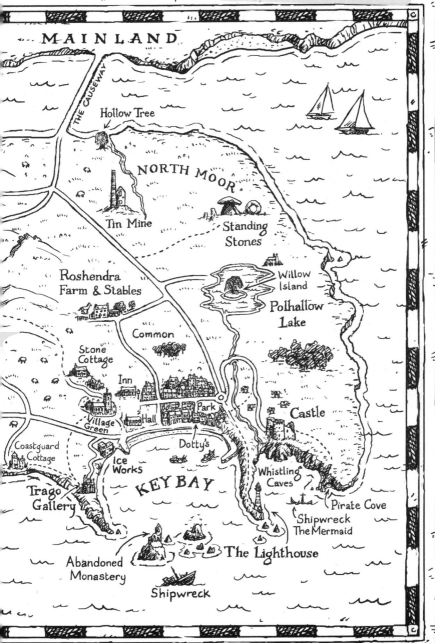

MAINLAND

THE CAUSEWAY

Hollow Tree

NORTH MOOR

Tin Mine

Standing Stones

Willow Island

Polhallow Lake

Roshendra Farm & Stables

Common

Stone Cottage

Inn

Village Green

Hall

Park

Dotty's

Castle

Coastguard Cottage

Ice Works

KEY BAY

Whistling Caves

Pirate Cove

Shipwreck The Mermaid

Trago Gallery

Abandoned Monastery

The Lighthouse

Shipwreck

Collect all the Adventure Island *books*

ADVENTURE ISLAND
THE MYSTERY OF THE
INVISIBLE SPY

Helen Moss

Illustrated by Leo Hartas

Orion
Children's Books

First published in Great Britain in 2012
by Orion Children's Books
a division of the Orion Publishing Group Ltd
Orion House
5 Upper St Martin's Lane
London WC2H 9EA
An Hachette UK company

1 3 5 7 9 10 8 6 4 2

Text copyright © Helen Moss 2012
Map and interior illustrations copyright © Leo Hartas 2012

The right of Helen Moss to be identified as
the author of this work has been asserted.

The Orion Publishing Group's policy is to use papers
that are natural, renewable and recyclable products and
made from wood grown in sustainable forests. The logging
and manufacturing processes are expected to conform to
the environmental regulations of the country of origin.

A catalogue record for this book
is available from the British Library.

ISBN 978 1 4440 0536 3

Printed in Great Britain by Clays Ltd, St Ives plc

For Jenny Savill,
Special Agent

One

Ambush!

E mily Wild checked her watch.
  The boys were late.

Scott and Jack's train – the 10.06 from London to
Penzance – had been due to arrive at Carrickstowe
Station seventeen minutes ago. Allowing five minutes
to get their bikes off the train and another ten to cycle
through town, they should be crossing the causeway
from the mainland to Castle Key precisely *now*!

Emily leaned back against the trunk of the willow tree and felt the ridges of warm bark through her t-shirt. The broad branch made a perfect observation post. Camouflaged by leafy fronds, you could monitor everyone entering or leaving the island across the causeway. Emily lowered the binoculars and wrote in the notebook propped open on her knees: *TESCO delivery van, 15.15.* That guy was running late too. Mrs Roberts at Lilac Cottage had her shopping delivered every Thursday afternoon and it usually arrived at ten past three.

'Maybe there's a traffic jam in Carrickstowe,' she said. 'What do you think, Drift?'

Drift was inside the hollow tree playing chicken with two very annoying squirrels. Every time he got close, they scurried up to a higher branch, taunting him and pulling faces. Drift perked one ear – the white one with brown spots – at Emily's words. He didn't know what she was saying, of course, but he was a very good listener.

'Jack's probably stopped to buy some sweets at the station kiosk,' Emily told him. 'Or they've got into a row over the quickest route to the causeway.' Emily didn't have any brothers or sisters herself, so when she'd first met Scott and Jack Carter she'd been a bit taken aback that arguing was their normal mode of communication. But that was a year ago and she was used to it now. Since then, they'd found buried treasure, discovered a new species of dinosaur, rescued a film star and tracked down a legendary cursed ruby, to name but a few of their adventures together.

Emily lifted the binoculars again, screwing up her eyes against the glare. The sun was sparkling off the waves in the channel between the island and the mainland; it bleached the sails of the yachts to a dazzling white and glinted off the wings of the gulls as they swooped. The tarmac road across the causeway shimmered in the heat haze. A green and yellow bus lumbered across, followed by a small silver car.

Emily did a double take. She cross-checked the registration number against yesterday's records. Yes, that was the same Ford Fiesta she'd seen three times in the last three days. She was pretty sure it didn't belong to anyone local. The driver was a young man on his own and Emily had never seen him talking to anyone. She'd spotted his car in some odd locations too. Once he was driving slowly along a moorland track near the quarry. And twice she'd seen him parked in a lay-by near Westward Beach. She was sure he'd sped off as soon as he noticed her glance in his direction as she cycled past.

Highly suspicious, Emily thought as she recorded the sighting in her notebook.

She picked up the binoculars again and, at last, she spotted two cyclists. Jack was in front, head down and legs pumping manically on the pedals of his BMX bike. Scott followed at a more leisurely pace, his floppy brown hair flying back in the breeze. A year older than Jack, Scott was more laid-back and – he liked to think – way cooler than his brother. Emily giggled. With their bulky backpacks, the boys looked like giant snails, carrying their homes on their backs.

She waited until the boys had left the causeway and were on the island road not far from the willow tree. Then she dangled her legs from the branch and dropped to the ground. Calling softly for Drift to follow, she commando-crawled through the bracken to the edge of the road.

'Stand and deliver!' she shouted as she leaped out of the undergrowth.

'Aggghhh!' Jack yelled, slamming his brakes on so hard they squealed. He'd been daydreaming about the gallons of ice-cold Coke he was going to knock back as soon as he got to Stone Cottage. Knowing Aunt Kate, she'd have some awesome cakes waiting for them too. Then they'd head off to The Lighthouse to see Emily and Drift. He had it all worked out. Then, all of a sudden, he was being set upon by a mugger and some kind of ferocious beast – quite possibly a mountain lion.

'Look what you're doing!' Scott shouted, almost crashing into him.

Jack opened his eyes and realized the ambushers were only Emily and Drift. He staggered onto the wide verge, dropped his bike against the hedge and with arms outstretched, keeled over backwards onto his rucksack in the long grass, sending up a cloud of fluffy white dandelion seeds. Drift bounced onto his stomach and licked his face in joyful greeting, as the seeds wafted around them like miniature parachutes.

'We saw you coming a mile off!' Jack spluttered through the tsunami of dog drool.

Scott flopped down next to him. 'Yeah, we were just *pretending* to be surprised!' he said, laughing as Drift belly-flopped onto his chest.

'Of course you were!' Emily laughed. She couldn't *stop* laughing, in fact, as the boys wriggled around like upturned beetles, pinned down by their heavy backpacks. When they finally managed to sit up she greeted them both with an awkward high-five-slash-hug. She quickly pulled away in case they thought she was being soppy. 'So what took you so long?' she asked. 'No, don't tell me. Jack stopped for sweets and then you couldn't agree which way to come.'

Jack stared at Emily and then at the pack of toffees he'd just pulled from his backpack. She was right! He *had* felt a bit peckish when they got off the train and had made a quick detour for emergency provisions. Then Scott refused to take a brilliant short-cut, just because it would involve lifting their bikes over a locked gate. Had Emily developed mind-reading powers since they'd last seen her?

Scott swigged from a bottle of water. 'You must've had your spies out watching us, Em!'

'I didn't need to!' Emily laughed. 'You two are just so predictable.'

'No, we're not!' Scott and Jack protested.

'Anyway, on the subject of spies,' Emily said, switching into a serious tone all of a sudden. 'I've spotted one.' She paused dramatically and looked from Jack to Scott and back again. 'Right here on Castle Key!'

Two

Counter Surveillance

J ack and Scott grinned at each other. They knew Emily was obsessed with espionage in all its forms, but this had to be a world record. They'd been on the island for less than ten minutes and she'd already presented them with a spy!

'So, what's his mission?' Scott asked in a mock-serious voice. 'Sussing out the secret ingredient in Dotty's Cornish pasties? Bugging Mrs Loveday's phone for enemy gossip?'

Emily ignored Scott's teasing. 'It's all in here,' she said, pulling her notebook from the shoulder bag where she kept her investigation kit. She proceeded to tell them all about the mysterious man in the silver Ford Fiesta.

'A *Ford Fiesta*!' Jack laughed. 'Aren't spies meant to drive Aston Martins or Ferraris kitted out with loads of gadgets and weapons?'

Scott rolled his eyes. 'You've been watching too many James Bond films! Real spies have to blend in to their surroundings.' But he couldn't help teasing Emily some more. 'Driving *slowly,* you say? Parking in *lay-bys*? That's pretty explosive stuff. Have you called this in to MI5 yet?'

Emily thumped his arm. 'You two don't have to help if you don't want to, but Drift and I are going to mount a full-scale counter-surveillance operation. We're starting at Westward Beach tomorrow morning, since that's where most of my sightings have been.'

Scott grinned. Westward Beach would be the perfect place to spend a hot summer's day. If Emily wanted to do a bit of snooping on Ford Fiesta Man while they were there, that was fine with him. 'We'll go deep undercover,' he said. 'We'll take our swimming things and snorkels and act like we're just having an ordinary day at the beach.'

'We'd better take a picnic as well,' Jack added, 'just to complete the disguise, of course!'

Drift wagged his tail. He recognized the word *beach,* and it was one of his favourites.

Emily smiled happily.

The boys were back and they had an investigation underway already!

—

Jack and Scott spent a quiet evening sitting round the weathered old pine table in the garden at Stone Cottage, chatting with Aunt Kate and tucking into a delicious pasta bake followed by banoffee pie. When they'd first come to stay with their great-aunt in Castle Key for the summer holidays they'd thought it was going to be the most boring six weeks ever. They were soon proved spectacularly wrong and had come back for every school holiday since, while Dad went off on his archaeological digs.

They were still eating as dusk fell. The buzz of insects bumbling among the lavender and rambling roses mingled with the mournful cries of seagulls perched on the chimney pots. Flowery scents wafted up on the warm salt air.

Yep, Jack thought sleepily. *It's good to be back in Castle Key.*

—

Next morning Emily called at Stone Cottage bright and early. They packed a picnic, Drift jumped into his special basket on the back of Emily's bike, and they set off for Westward Beach.

The sun was already beating down from a cloudless sky as they cycled along the dusty road over South Moor. By the time they reached the beach the friends were all ready for a swim. They dashed over the hot sand and charged into the waves, laughing and shrieking as the cold water crashed over them.

But it wasn't long before Emily was getting on with the business of the day, scoping out the best vantage point for the surveillance operation. She found a spot on a rocky outcrop halfway along the beach, with a view along the seafront in both directions. She lifted the binoculars to her eyes, under cover of a wide-brimmed straw hat. 'I'll take first watch,' she said.

'I'll take first sandwich,' Jack offered, settling down on a flat sun-baked rock.

The beach was getting busy. Families were setting up camp with sunshades, windbreaks and picnic blankets. Everywhere people were paddling, playing Frisbee and building sandcastles.

Scott took the next turn on watch. After fifteen minutes he handed the binoculars to Jack. 'Number of spies observed? Zero!' he laughed.

Jack was zooming in on the ice-cream van at the edge of the parking area, sizing up the length of the queue, when he noticed a small silver car cruising along the seafront. It was a Ford Fiesta. And, yes, it was pulling into the car park. Almost dropping the binoculars with excitement he read the number plate out loud.

'Yes,' Emily whistled under her breath. 'That's him.'

Scott was sprawled out on the warm rock with his hands laced behind his head. He'd been woken far too early for the first day of the holidays. 'So what's he doing?' he asked with a yawn. 'Applying sun lotion in a suspicious manner?'

'He's getting out of the car,' Jack whispered. He watched the 'spy' stroll northwards along the seafront, and made a mental note of his appearance – he knew Emily would test him on it later: a tall man with a baseball cap over straight dark hair, rounded shoulders beneath a grey t-shirt with a black and white bird logo on the back, knobbly knees, mushroom-white legs poking out from khaki shorts, ankle socks and chunky hiking sandals. A pair of binoculars and a serious-looking camera bounced on his chest.

'Come on,' Emily whispered. 'Let's tail him. Pretend we're walking up to the road.'

'We *are* walking up to the road,' Scott pointed out as they climbed the sandy wooden steps from the beach.

Scott, Jack, Emily and Drift followed their target at a safe distance. He strode past the grand Victorian mansions that lined the seafront, set back behind wrought iron gates and gloomy conifer hedges, and kept heading north beyond the end of the beach where a derelict pier jutted out into the sea. Jack shuddered. There was something very sinister about that pier. He wouldn't like to go near it on a dark night!

Emily noticed Jack's reaction. 'Spooky, isn't it?' she whispered. 'There used to be a posh resort and spa here in Victorian times. But there was a massive fire on the pier and someone was killed, so the council shut it down years ago.' Suddenly she stopped, pretending to look for something in her bag.

The man had turned off to the right, heading into the sand dunes.

The friends hurried to the point where the 'spy' had left the road. Jack gazed inland. Wave upon wave of pale sand, dotted with clumps of marram grass, and criss-crossed by rabbit paths, gradually gave way to heathland, cloaked with purple and yellow wildflowers. He hoped Emily wasn't getting ideas about following the man into the dunes. It was almost midday and the sand was as hot as melted mozzarella on a pizza.

But suddenly Scott was pointing. 'Look, there he is!'

The man had doubled back and was now clambering up a dune behind the mansions, leaving ogre-sized footprints in the loose sand. Eventually he reached the top, where he disappeared into a small wooden hut.

Scott raised his eyebrows. 'What's that? Some kind of military look out post?'

Emily didn't answer. Instead, she surveyed the territory. 'There's another hut at the bottom of that dune over there. If we're quick we can reach it before he spots us. Come on!'

Three

Operation Skylark

Before Jack had time to object Emily was darting off, her bare feet spraying up plumes of sand. Drift and Scott ran after her. Jack had no choice but to follow. He dived into what looked like a garden shed and collapsed in a hot-and-bothered heap.

'Youch!' he yelped, as a splinter the size of a tree trunk flaked off from the rough wooden floor, pierced the seat of his shorts and embedded itself in his bottom.

Scott and Emily took no notice.

Jack sat up and looked around. The shed was empty apart from a few stools tucked under a shelf along one side. A row of slots like elongated letterboxes had been cut into the wall at eye level.

Emily was already pointing the binoculars out towards the hut at the top of the dune.

But Scott started laughing. 'I think we can drop the surveillance mission now, Em. I've just worked it out – these huts are bird hides, aren't they? Looks like your "spy" is a birdwatcher!'

'A *birdwatcher*?' Jack said. 'What do you mean?'

Scott rolled his eyes. 'Duh! A person who watches birds. The clue's in the name!'

'But birds don't *do* anything,' Jack snorted. 'They just fly around and lay eggs and stuff.'

Scott shrugged 'Well, some people think they're interesting. These huts are here so you can watch without disturbing them. Keen birdwatchers bring a flask and sandwiches and stay all day.'

'Wow, they really know how to have a good time, don't they?' Jack said sarcastically, kicking at an old biscuit wrapper in the corner. *Digestives,* he thought. These birdwatchers even had boring biscuits! 'If you think I'm going to sit in a boiling hot shed all day, watching some bloke staring at seagulls and scoffing sandwiches, think again!'

'Nobody *forced* you to come on this mission!' Emily

snapped, her temper frayed by disappointment. The man wasn't a spy! How could she have missed the signs? That bird on his t-shirt was the logo of the Royal Society for the Protection of Birds, for goodness' sake, and Castle Key was famous for its rare seabirds! All that driving around and parking in odd places? He'd obviously just been looking for a good spot to sight a cormorant or a chough.

Emily was still staring despondently through the viewing slot when she caught sight of a plump brown bird fluttering down to a nest in a dip among the grass on a sandy ledge. It dangled a worm over the gaping orange beaks of three downy chicks. Emily knew enough about birds to recognize a family of skylarks. She pointed them out to Scott and handed him the binoculars, just as the lark did a vertical take-off. They watched spellbound, as it hovered high above the nest, pouring out a bubbling waterfall of song for minutes on end, before sky-diving back to the chicks.

'Wow, that was pretty cool!' Scott whistled. 'Like a bird opera or something. Shame you missed it down there,' he told Jack, who was writhing around on the floor trying to extract the splinter from his bottom. Unfortunately Drift thought it was a game and kept pouncing on him.

'Tragic!' Jack muttered. There was no way *he* was going to turn into a birdwatcher!

Emily looked through the slot and saw the man leave the other bird hide and head back towards the seafront. 'I suppose we might as well go, too,' she sighed.

'Good idea,' Jack agreed. 'Back to the beach for ice creams.'

'Of course, he *could* still be a spy . . .' Emily said hopefully.

'Read my lips,' Jack said. 'The Man Is Not A Spy!'

Emily frowned. 'Maybe we should follow him one more time. You know, just in case?'

As Jack was taking Emily by the arm and frog-marching her towards the door, Scott noticed a logbook on the shelf. The dog-eared pages were full of notes about all the birds that people had seen from the hide. He glanced at the most recent comment: *Superb pair of skylarks with late brood in nest.* It was signed *Otto and Karin, Frankfurt.*

Suddenly he thought of a way to prove to Emily, once and for all, that Ford Fiesta Man was a genuine birdwatcher and *not* a spy. Then she might let the subject drop at last. 'You go on,' he told the others. 'I'll catch you up.'

Scott ran up the dune and into the bird hide at the top. He grabbed the logbook and flicked through to the latest record. As he'd expected, it was also about the skylarks. *Excellent sighting of pair of nesting larks on ledge. Male in full song-flight. Don't miss it!*

Scott was about to photograph the evidence to show

Emily when he stopped, his phone still halfway out of his jeans pocket.

The person who'd recorded that song-flight was *not* Ford Fiesta Man!

The comment was dated two days ago and signed by *Jenny Sanders, Toronto, Canada*.

Scott felt excitement prickle the back of his neck. If their man was such a keen birdwatcher, why hadn't he made a note of the fabulous display that they'd just witnessed? He ran to the viewing window and looked out. There was a perfect view of the skylark nest with its three noisy little chicks. There was no way the man could have missed it. And yet, there was no entry in the logbook for today!

Maybe Emily was onto something after all?

Come to think of it, with those brand new khaki shorts and the socks and sandals and the RSPB t-shirt, didn't Ford Fiesta Man look as if he was trying just a *bit* too hard? It was almost as if he was *deliberately* dressed to play the part of a birdwatcher.

But if he wasn't watching skylarks, what *was* he spying on from the hide in the sand dunes?

Back on the seafront Jack bought an ice cream. He bought one for Emily, too, to try to cheer her up. It didn't work. She clattered around, packing away the picnic things and shaking the towels so hard she was in danger of shaking the patterns off along with the sand.

'What's Scott *doing* up there?' Jack wondered out loud. 'If he's suddenly decided to take up birdwatching, I'm never talking to him again. It'll be trainspotting and stamp collecting next!'

Emily attempted a smile but couldn't pull it off. Losing her spy was just too depressing. But when she looked up she saw Scott jogging towards them, leaping over sandcastles and hurdling deckchairs.

'Newsflash,' he puffed as he reached the rocks. 'He's *not* a birdwatcher!'

Jack and Emily gaped at Scott in confusion.

'He didn't write up the skylark song-flight in the logbook.'

Jack shrugged. 'Big deal! Nor did we!'

'That's exactly the point. We weren't there to watch the birds, either!'

Jack wasn't convinced, but Emily beamed at Scott as if he'd just found the cure for the common cold. She nodded so furiously that her long brown curls bounced around her face.

'I knew it!' She turned to Jack. 'If that guy knew *anything* about birds he wouldn't have missed that skylark display. It'd be like going to a Formula One race and not noticing who won.'

'Well, if you put it like that,' Jack conceded with a grin. He still wasn't totally buying in to Scott's logbook theory, but at least it had stopped Emily shaking towels to within an inch of their lives. In fact, she'd perked up so much she'd got her notebook out and was writing a heading on a new page:

OPERATION SKYLARK.

Then she took out her ruler and underlined it twice.

Four

Paparazzi

Back at Stone Cottage, Scott and Jack were hardly though the door when Aunt Kate called from the kitchen, asking them to pop into the village for her. 'I'm making a chocolate cake and I've just run out of eggs!'

'Jack'll get them,' Scott called. 'I'm going for a shower.'

Before Jack could argue, Scott had disappeared into the bathroom. Jack didn't want to stand in the way of a chocolate cake, so he hopped back onto his bike and set off for the mini-market on Castle Key high street.

He was almost there when he spotted a familiar vehicle parked outside the newsagent – *the silver Ford Fiesta!*

Jack slipped into an alleyway and kept watch. *I've definitely been spending too much time with Emily*, he thought. *I'm going into stealth mode for a guy who's probably more interested in seagulls than surveillance.* After a few minutes Ford Fiesta Man emerged from the newsagent with a paper under his arm. He pulled his baseball cap down over his eyes, looked over his shoulder and then disappeared into the mini-market.

OK, Jack thought, *I'm going in!* He sauntered into the shop, grabbed a basket and did his casually-buying-some-eggs act as he followed the man up and down the aisles.

Instant noodles (one extra-large pot), Jack noted. *Tortilla chips (one pack), spicy salsa (small jar), milk (one pint) and teabags (small pack).* Using his awesome powers of deduction, Jack figured out a full profile of his target: he lived alone and he'd not signed up to the five-a-day healthy eating message. *Excellent intelligence gathering, Agent Carter*, he told himself. Then he ducked behind the chocolate-bar display and watched the man pay for his purchases.

'Are you settling in alright?' Mrs McElroy asked from behind the counter.

'Fine, thank you,' the man mumbled, handing over his money and hurrying out with a quick, 'Bye!'

Just my luck he's not the chatty type, Jack thought. He waited until Ford Fiesta Man had left and then sauntered up to the counter. 'Er, do you know who that was?'

Mrs McElroy shut the drawer of the cash register. 'Yes, dear. That's Mr Rudge. Why did you want to know?'

Jack stared at Mrs McElroy as if hypnotized by her bifocal glasses. *Good question! Why* did *he want to know?* He felt in his pocket and tugged out a scrap of paper. 'It's just that he dropped this. I thought it might be important. I could, er, you know, take it back to him.'

Mrs McElroy smiled at Jack as if he'd sprouted a halo and angel wings. 'What a considerate young man! Mr Rudge has just rented our holiday cottage at Polhallow Lake for the week. He's here for the birds. Keeps himself to himself, but seems nice enough . . .'

Jack mumbled his thanks, stuffed the piece of paper – which he noticed was a two-for-one offer on takeaway pizza – back into his pocket and scooted out of the shop. He was so pleased with himself he practically skipped home to Stone Cottage. He couldn't wait to see Scott and Emily's faces. This was so much better than Scott's feeble logbook evidence! He had a name for their mystery spy. He had his address. He even had his dinner menu!

In fact, Jack realized as he pushed open the front door and saw Aunt Kate in the kitchen, the only thing he *didn't* have was eggs!

He turned on his heel and headed back to the shop.

—

Next morning the friends stationed themselves on the rocks at Westward Beach once again.

Scott and Emily had been awe-struck by Jack's intelligence-gathering skills of the previous evening – so much so, that Scott was convinced Jack was making the whole thing up – until Emily confirmed that Mr and Mrs McElroy did indeed own a small holiday cottage near Polhallow Lake.

'He *must* be a spy!' Emily said happily. 'Why else would he be passing himself off as a birdwatcher, when he doesn't even notice a skylark doing its *Britain's Got Talent* audition right in front of his nose?'

They took turns to watch the road and car park, but, disappointingly, the silver Ford Fiesta didn't appear. They were on the point of giving up when Emily spotted Rudge getting out of a different car – a black Toyota – and hurrying off towards the sand dunes.

'Ha! He's *obviously* changed vehicles to shake off anyone who's trying to tail him,' Emily said knowledgeably. 'Well, he isn't fooling *us* with such a basic ploy!'

Rudge was in his birdwatching outfit again, but this time he skirted the edge of the dunes, and took up position in a deep hollow. The friends followed and watched from behind a stand of tangled hawthorn bushes.

After a few minutes the huge zoom lens of Rudge's camera poked out like a sniper's gun.

'What's he doing?' Scott whispered. 'All he can see from there is the gardens of those old mansions on the seafront.'

When Rudge finally left, the friends crept to the hollow. Scott was right. The view was of high wooden fences and evergreen hedges enclosing two large back gardens. Sounds of building work – the whine of a saw and the thud of a hammer – came from behind the fence of one garden, and through the hedge of the other it was just possible to glimpse striped sunshades and the turquoise shimmer of a swimming pool.

'Nice pad!' Jack remarked. 'Who lives there?'

'An actress called Tamara Bradshaw,' Emily said.

'You mean the glamorous one who's been in all the soaps?' Scott asked. 'No wonder Rudge is lurking with his zoom lens. He's obviously taking sneaky shots of Tamara Bradshaw in her garden to sell to the papers!'

'So that's the kind of *bird* he's watching!' Jack laughed. 'The kind that lies by the pool in a bikini!'

Emily was mortified. If it turned out she'd been following some creepy paparazzi photographer, the boys would never let her live it down! Well, she wasn't going to give up on her spy that easily. 'There's one way to find out,' she said, marching across the dunes to the road. 'We'll go and ask.'

'What?' Jack spluttered. 'We just rock up at Tamara Bradshaw's door and say "Excuse us, Tammy, but have you been out sunbathing in skimpy swimwear this morning?"'

'Of course not!' Emily said crossly. 'We'll pretend we're autograph hunters.'

Drift and the boys followed her up a sweeping gravel drive to a gleaming black front door set between white marble columns.

Emily rang the bell. The door was answered by a middle-aged woman in a flowery skirt and faded blue top. When Emily mumbled something about autographs, she put down a washing basket, smiled and shook her head. 'Sorry. Tamara's at her other house in LA. I'm the housekeeper.'

'Do you know when she'll be back?' Scott asked politely.

'She's away all summer. I don't blame her, with all that racket going on next door.'

The housekeeper was right. The sawing and hammering they'd noticed at the back was even louder here.

'Ooh, is someone famous moving in?' Jack asked.

The housekeeper was already closing the door. 'Sorry,

love. It's just some old chap. Retired gardener, I think. He's doing the place up.'

The friends trudged back down the drive and onto the seafront. 'No wonder old Rudge wasn't interested in skylarks,' Jack grumbled. 'He's just a celebrity photographer.'

'A pretty hopeless one too, since the celebrity isn't even at home,' Scott added.

Suddenly Emily stopped and grabbed the boys' arms. She whipped a map out of her bag and pretended to study it. 'I think the beach is this way!' she announced in a loud voice. Then under her breath she hissed, 'Don't look now! What's the guy in the ice-cream van up to?'

Five

Ice-Cream Spy

Of course Jack *did* look at the guy in the ice-cream van.

The pink and white Mr Whippy van was stationed near the steps to the beach, exactly as it had been the previous day. True, it was a different person serving – a pale chubby-faced guy with heavy square glasses. Yesterday, Jack remembered being served by a pretty teenaged girl with a ponytail and a strappy top that revealed a massive butterfly tattoo on her shoulder. But surely even Emily couldn't find anything suspicious about different people working different days.

'What?' he demanded.

'He's taking photos!' Emily whispered from behind the map.

Now Scott sneaked a glance too. The ice-cream man had a mobile phone in his hand. He was probably just reading a text message. But no, maybe Emily was right. He was holding the phone out and he kept glancing up at the house over the road.

Scott looked at the house – Sunset Lodge, according to a fading brass sign on the gatepost. It was the one with all the building work going on. Why would anyone want photos of a ramshackle old mansion half-covered in scaffolding and surrounded by builders' vans and cement mixers?

An old man in a short-sleeved shirt and brown cord trousers ambled out onto the drive from the overgrown garden. He was carrying a hedge-trimmer and wearing gardening gloves.

Retired gardener, Scott thought, remembering the housekeeper's words.

As the man stooped to stroke a scrawny little tabby cat, his thick, white hair fell across his forehead.

The ice-cream man held his phone up again.

'Maybe Rudge wasn't trying to get pictures of

Tamara Bradshaw, after all,' Emily whispered. 'Perhaps he's staking out that old man at Sunset Lodge for some reason, and maybe the ice-cream guy is working *with* him. Let's go and talk to him.'

'Good idea.' Jack said. He was sure Emily's theory was nothing but wishful thinking, but it was hotter than ever and an ice cream was just what he needed. He hurried to the van and studied the price list. He gave the Cornettos his serious consideration, but finally plumped for a large cone with a flake. This was the kind of undercover operation he liked!

'Is this a good spot for selling ice creams?' Scott asked in his best casual-conversation voice.

The man didn't look up from spiralling soft, white ice cream into the cone. 'It's alright.' He spoke with a lisp, barely opening his mouth, as if reluctant to waste his breath.

Emily ordered two small cones, one for herself and one for Drift. 'Do you like selling ice creams?' she asked.

'It's alright,' the man grunted. He wiped his hands down the front of his jacket. It was one of those white lab coats favoured by mad scientists, butchers and ice-cream sellers. Although the man was very chubby, Jack noticed that the wrists that slid out from his sleeves were thin and knobbly.

Behind his thick glasses the man's eyes flicked towards Sunset Lodge. Jack followed his gaze. A builder was unloading a toolkit from the van. The old gardener had disappeared behind the hedge again.

Having run out of small-talk options, the friends wandered back along the beach in silence – their mouths full of ice cream and their heads full of questions. Was the surly ice-cream seller the fake birdwatcher's accomplice? And why would anyone want pictures of a retired gardener anyway?

Suddenly Jack stopped. 'That's the girl who was in the ice-cream van yesterday.' He pointed to a girl of about seventeen with a blonde ponytail, lounging in a deckchair with her feet up. She was reading a book entitled *Rainforest Lepidoptera* and twizzling a pink flip-flop on her big toe.

'Are you sure?' Scott asked.

The girl lowered her book and leaned forward to take a drink from a bottle of water, revealing a bikini top and a tattoo of a giant butterfly stretching its wings across her shoulder blade. Jack nodded. She wasn't exactly easy to miss!

'Brilliant!' Emily whispered. 'Maybe she can give us some information.' She marched over to the deckchair. 'Excuse me, is that your ice-cream van?'

The girl unplugged her iPod from one ear. 'Yeah. Well, it's my dad's.'

'Oh, is that your dad in the van now?' Jack asked.

'What, that weirdo? Don't make me laugh!' The girl

peered over her sunglasses. 'You're not Health and Safety, are you?'

'Of course not,' Scott said. 'He, er, just looks a bit like someone we know.'

'You said he was a weirdo?' Emily asked.

'Truth is,' the girl chuckled, 'I've never seen him before in my life. He just wandered up to the van. He said, "I'll give you fifty quid to let me have a go at selling ice creams for a couple of hours!" And I jumped at the chance!'

The friends all stared at her in disbelief. 'No way!' Jack whistled.

The girl wiped away tears of laughter. 'Yes, way! He said it's something he's always wanted to do! I shouldn't have let him really because he's not had the proper training, but why turn down free money and a chance to put my feet up?'

'And you don't know anything else about him?' Emily pressed.

'He's a nutcase if you ask me!' The girl tapped the side of her head. 'But he seems harmless enough.' She looked up and noticed Jack staring at her butterfly tattoo. 'Do you like it?'

Jack blushed. 'Er, yeah, it's lovely.'

The girl smiled. 'It's a Queen Alexandra Birdwing – the biggest butterfly in the world. One day I'm going to New Guinea to see them in the wild – if I can save enough money.' She held up her book.

'*Lepidoptera* is the fancy name for butterflies and moths.'

For once Jack was lost for words. 'Awesome!' he mumbled.

—

'That proves it! The ice-cream guy has got to be working with Rudge!' Emily said excitedly as soon as they were out of earshot. 'Why else would he just turn up and ask to sell ice creams? They're staking out Sunset Lodge!'

'I agree,' Scott said. 'But why?'

'No, he's not working *with* Rudge,' Jack suddenly blurted. 'He *is* Rudge!'

'But he doesn't look anything like Rudge!' Scott pointed out. 'OK, he could have put on those glasses and the white coat, but Rudge is dead skinny and the ice cream guy is, well, not to put too fine a point on it, he's fat.'

'No, he's not fat!' Jack retorted.

Scott laughed. It wasn't like his brother to be sensitive about such things. 'OK, not *fat*. Let's call him plump . . .'

Jack shook his head. 'No, the man in the van is not fat at all – or plump or stocky or portly or stout. He's thin! He must be wearing a fat suit under that white coat, and padding in his cheeks!' He puffed up his cheeks like a hamster to demonstrate. 'But did you notice his wrists and his hands? They were dead skinny.'

Emily smiled slowly. Then she grabbed Jack by the elbows and jumped up and down. 'Jack, you're a genius!'

Scott wouldn't go that far but he had to admit Jack was right for once! He joined the victory dance. Drift bounced round and round them in circles, splashing in the lace-edged waves that were beginning to rush in over the sand.

At last they headed back to the rocks, continuing to discuss their breakthrough as they walked.

'So we know Rudge is staking out Sunset Lodge from the ice-cream van . . .' Emily said.

Scott thought for a moment. 'Of course, that's what he was up to in the dunes. He wasn't snooping on Tamara Bradshaw. It was the back garden of Sunset Lodge he was interested in.'

'But why?' Emily asked for the hundredth time. 'If that old guy's just a retired gardener!'

'What if Rudge is a *gardening* spy?' Jack suggested. 'He could be one of those dead keen ones who do the Chelsea Flower Show and stuff. Perhaps the guy at Sunset Lodge has invented a new kind of rose bush or something and Rudge wants to get his hands on the secret . . .'

Scott laughed. 'Like Alan Titchmarsh meets James Bond, you mean?'

Emily laughed too, but then she shook her head. 'I don't think this has anything to do with roses . . .'

Back at the rocks Jack, Scott and Drift fished in the tide pools, while Emily took her notebook from her bag and turned to a new page. She wasn't sure what this case was about yet, but she was determined to find out. People didn't go around impersonating birdwatchers and ice-cream sellers for no reason! Beneath the heading OPERATION SKYLARK she wrote *Ice cream spy* and added three question marks. She was brushing stray grains of sand from the page when she felt the chill of a shadow slide across her body.

She looked up to see a tall figure towering over her.

Backlit by the dazzling sunshine, Emily couldn't make out who it was for a moment.

Then she saw that it was Rudge. He'd dumped the white coat and the fat suit.

And this time he wasn't holding out an ice-cream cone.

Six

A Matter of National Security

'So,' Rudge said in a voice as cold as ice cream, 'Would you kids mind telling me *exactly* what you think you're up to?'

Right back at you, Jack thought. The man looked about to blow a fuse. His brows were scrunched down into a V shape and a muscle twitched along his cheekbone. Jack had seen that look before – most recently on the face of Mr Jellicoe, his art teacher, following the incident with the red paint, the trainer on a broom handle and the footprints on the ceiling.

'What are we *doing*?' Jack asked in his most innocent voice. 'Just enjoying the sea air. Why?'

'You know perfectly well why! All those questions at the ice-cream van. You're *following* me, aren't you?' Rudge's gaze dropped to Emily's notebook. She snapped it shut but the damage was already done. Rudge had obviously perfected the art of long-distance upside-down reading. '*Ice cream spy?*' He spat the words out like machine-gun fire.

The three friends all spoke at once.

'No!' Jack protested, adopting his first rule of defence: *deny everything!*

'No!' said Scott.

'Yes!' said Emily.

The boys gaped at her. Were they hearing things or had Emily really just blown their cover wide open?

Emily, meanwhile, was staring up at Rudge, her eyes gleaming. 'I've just figured it out,' she breathed. She scrambled to her feet and looked up and down the beach to make sure no one was listening. 'You're from MI5, aren't you?' She dropped her voice even lower. 'Is that old man at Sunset Lodge an enemy agent?'

Scott made a strangled noise and sank his head in

his hands. Jack held his breath waiting for Rudge to (a) fall over laughing, (b) call the police, or (c) suggest Emily have her head examined. But to his amazement, Rudge was silent for a few moments, as if calculating his next move. Then he sank down on the rocks. He slowly reached up, took off his heavy glasses and extracted two rolls of white padding from inside his mouth. 'That's better,' he said, now without the lisp.

'So, you're not really an ice-cream seller, Mr Rudge?' Scott asked politely, trying to demonstrate that, unlike Emily, he was a rational *sane* human being who didn't go around raving about MI5 and enemy agents.

Rudge shook his head and smiled. Without the scowl and the padding, his face was quite pleasant, with a wide, crooked smile – although his skin was still too pale, like a plant that had grown in the dark. 'I'm not a birdwatcher, either,' he said, glancing down at the socks and sandals. 'This isn't my usual look.'

'Are you a newspaper photographer?' Jack asked

Rudge rested his elbows on his knees and cracked the knuckles of both hands. 'Nope!' he said, shading his eyes and gazing out to sea, as if noticing it for the first time. 'Why have you been stalking me?' He seemed more perplexed than angry now.

Emily gave a mysterious smile. 'Let's just say I noticed a pattern of behaviour that alerted me to your activities.'

Rudge raised an eyebrow. 'How did you know I wasn't a birdwatcher?'

'You didn't notice the skylarks,' Scott said.

'What skylarks?'

'Exactly!' Emily couldn't keep the triumph out of her voice.

Rudge frowned. 'And you saw through my disguise in the ice-cream van?'

Jack nodded. 'You've got skinny hands.'

Rudge turned his hands over and contemplated his palms. 'And how did you find out my name?'

'I kind of overheard it in the shop last night,' Jack admitted.

'Well, I have to say, your surveillance skills are most impressive.'

Emily glowed with pride. Forget *pretty* or *smart* or *charming*; *impressive surveillance skills* was the highest compliment anyone could ever pay her. 'Of course, Rudge isn't your real name, is it?' she whispered. 'It's the identity MI5 have given you for this operation!'

Rudge didn't speak for a moment. Then he looked up suddenly as if he'd come to an important decision. 'We can't talk here any longer.' He glanced at his watch. 'Wait fifteen minutes then walk to the viewpoint at the south end of the beach. I'll be sitting on the bench. If I raise my binoculars twice that means the coast is clear. If not, go straight past and await further communications.' Then he stood up and strode off down the beach.

The friends stared at each other in stunned silence.

Jack was the first to speak. 'Butterfly Girl was right. He's a total fruit loop!'

'He's MI5,' Emily replied. 'I bet you a million pounds.'

'Like you've *got* a million pounds!' Jack snorted. 'Scott, tell Em she's crazy!'

'No! Tell Jack *he's* crazy!' Emily fired back.

They both stared at Scott, waiting to see which way he would jump.

Scott suspected Jack was right. Why would an agent from the British intelligence agency be wandering around in Castle Key? On the other hand, he was definitely up to *some* sort of covert operation. 'Let's go and see what he has to say. Then we'll decide who's crazy around here.'

The friends watched the seconds tick by on Emily's watch. The wait seemed more like fifteen hours than fifteen minutes but at last it was time to move. They strolled as casually as they could to the end of the beach.

'There he is,' Emily said out of the corner of her mouth, looking up to the viewpoint, which stood on a small headland. A lonely figure sitting on the bench raised his binoculars and lowered them. They all held their breath waiting for the second part of the signal.

'Yes!' Emily breathed as the figure raised the binoculars to his eyes once more.

They climbed the winding path to the viewpoint and gathered round the low stone pillar, pretending to inspect the metal plaque on the top. It was engraved with arrows, like the points of a compass, showing the direction and distance of famous landmarks around the world.

Scott began to read them out. '*Eiffel Tower, three hundred and fifty-five miles. Mount Everest, four thousand, eight hundred and . . .*'

Moments later, Rudge got up from the bench and joined them. He gazed down at the pillar as if fascinated by fact that it was 2,759 miles to the North Pole. 'Before I can reveal the nature of my operation,' he said finally, 'you must all swear to absolute secrecy. This is a matter of national security.'

Emily thought she might just explode with excitement. This was her birthday, Christmas and Bonfire Night all rolled into one. Scott and Jack were hooked now too. *A matter of national security!* What could possibly be more thrilling than that?

'Of course!' the friends whispered in unison.

There was another long pause. When Rudge spoke his voice was hushed. 'As you suspected, I am an MI5 agent. My codename is London Eye.'

'Cool!' Jack whistled.

Scott glanced at Emily. He could almost see the words *Told you so* hovering over her head in a giant thought bubble. But he had to admit, she'd been right all along! And this *was* pretty exciting!

'I have the owner of Sunset Lodge under surveillance,' Rudge went on.

'The retired gardener?' Scott asked.

'That's just his legend, isn't it?' Emily asked.

Rudge twitched an eyebrow. 'That's right.'

'His *legend*?' Jack echoed.

'That's what the intelligence agencies call a cover story,' Emily explained, thrilled to be using a word she'd only read about in books.

Rudge nodded. 'He's going under the name of Edward Pym.'

'So who is he really?' Jack asked eagerly. 'A Russian agent or something?'

Rudge nodded slowly. 'We believe that "Edward Pym" has been working for the Russian secret service for almost forty years.' Rudge placed his bony hands on the pillar and slumped forward, as if the thought of Pym's activities was draining his energy. 'His real name is thought to be Vladimir Kiev, but he has several other identities, including that of a German banker called Karl Eiffel. He is fluent in English, of course, as well as many other languages. He's known to British intelligence as Kremlin.'

'Awesome!' Jack breathed.

Rudge continued. 'Travelling in the guise of an international oil tycoon, Kremlin has channelled top-secret British military and strategic information to the Russian secret service . . .'

'The KGB?' Scott asked, remembering the name from an old spy film.

Rudge nodded. 'Yes, although it's not called that any more. Kremlin was a major player throughout the Cold War – nuclear missiles, the Korean War, the space race . . . He was leaking secrets to the Soviet Union the whole time. More recently he's been responsible for the loss of two of our best agents in the Middle East. We suspect he still has links with various terrorist organizations. If Pym *is* who we think he is, he's an extremely dangerous man.'

'Can't you just get the police to arrest him?' Jack asked.

Emily shot him a pitying look. 'It's obviously not that easy.' She turned to Rudge. 'I'm sure you have to take a lot of complex operational factors into consideration.'

Jack and Scott shared a secret eye roll. Emily was being a real teacher's pet!

Rudge smiled at Emily as if she'd just handed her homework in a day early. 'That's right. If Kremlin suspects that MI5 are on to him, the Russians will spirit him out of here before you can say *Russian Roulette*.'

Emily glanced sideways at Rudge, biting her lip, plucking up courage to ask the question that had been bursting to get out since the moment she'd heard the magical words, *I am an MI5 agent*. 'Could *we* help?' she asked nervously.

Help? Scott thought. *KGB, nuclear missiles, terrorist organizations* . . . this was serious stuff. How exactly could they help with that?

He nearly fell off the headland with surprise at Rudge's reply.

'You know, I think maybe you could . . .'

Seven

The Seagull has Landed

Rudge studied Emily, Scott and Jack with narrowed eyes, as if gauging their trustworthiness. 'I need proof positive that Edward Pym is Agent Kremlin before my boss at MI5 will give the go-ahead for a raid, but it's difficult to get close enough. It's highly likely that at least one of those builders at Sunset Lodge is a bodyguard – probably an ex-KGB agent.'

Emily nodded. It all made sense. She'd already noted

57

that none of the builders' vans belonged to local builders like Pete Morley.

'A bunch of kids hanging around is much less likely to arouse suspicion than I am,' Rudge went on. 'You might be able to get closer.'

'What do you mean by proof positive?' Scott asked.

'We know that Kremlin sustained a serious wound to his right hand during an explosion in Casablanca in 1992. If Pym *is* our man, he'll have extensive scarring, possibly several missing fingers. That's the evidence I need.'

Scott pictured the old man stroking the cat on the drive. In spite of the heat, Pym had been wearing gloves. Was he just an ordinary gardener protecting his hands from thorns? Or did he have something to hide?

'Mission understood!' Emily said, scribbling furiously in her notebook. 'We'll acquire top-quality photographic evidence for you.' For a moment Scott thought she was going to stand to attention and salute.

Rudge nodded. 'Ground rules: you tell nobody about this operation and there is to be no contact with the target.'

'Of course,' Scott said. 'How do we let you know when we've found something?'

'It's vital that we're not seen together again,' Rudge explained. 'Kremlin's guards may already be watching us.'

'We need an isolated location where we can leave a

message without being seen,' Emily said earnestly. 'It's called a dead drop,' she explained to the boys.

'What about in one of the other bird hides on the island?' Scott suggested.

'Brilliant idea,' Emily agreed. 'There's one on North Moor near the old tin mine.'

'We could leave a coded message in the logbook.' Scott was really getting into the role of secret agent now. 'You know, like *The Seagull has Landed*.'

Rudge nodded. 'OK. That means I can stick with my birdwatcher disguise, too. I'll lie low and check for a message two days from now.'

'We'll have to use steganography,' Emily said.

Jack grinned. 'What's that? Something to do with dinosaurs?'

Scott rolled his eyes. 'That's *stegosaurus*, you wombat!'

'Steganography means hidden writing,' Emily said. 'You hide the real message inside one that looks perfectly ordinary. You just need to know a key, like a sequence of numbers, to tell you which letters make up the hidden message.' She looked at Rudge expectantly. 'A *sequence of numbers*!' she repeated.

'Oh, yes, of course,' Rudge said. 'Let's use, er, one-eight-two-five.'

'Only four digits?' Emily asked. 'Is that secure enough?'

Rudge sighed. Jack knew how he felt. Emily could be

very persistent. 'It's plenty,' he said. 'We don't want to overcomplicate things.'

'No, of course not,' Emily agreed. She picked up her pen to jot down the numbers.

Rudge shook his head. 'Don't write it down. In fact, I'm going to have to ask you to destroy that notebook.'

Scott and Jack looked at each other. *Destroy her beloved notebook?* Emily was going to have a hissy fit!

But Emily nodded seriously. 'I understand. It could fall into enemy hands.'

'What are our codenames?' Jack asked suddenly. He'd seen enough spy films to know that they *had* to have codenames.

'You guys really know your stuff, don't you?' Rudge said with a smile. 'I was just coming to that. He looked across to the rocks where Drift was stalking seagulls. 'Why don't we stick to the bird theme? You be Seagull One.' Then he pointed to Scott and Emily. 'And Seagull Two and Seagull Three.'

Emily couldn't help feeling that she should be Seagull One, since this whole mission had been her idea in the first place, but she thought it might sound unprofessional to point it out.

And anyway Agent London Eye was already walking away.

Emily couldn't sleep that night. She lay awake in her little circular bedroom on the top floor of The Lighthouse – which her parents ran as a Bed and Breakfast – reliving every glorious moment of the day's events. '*Impressive surveillance skills,*' she whispered to Drift, who was curled up in the crook of her knees. 'Agent London Eye said that!'

Drift twitched an ear and snored contentedly.

Emily didn't mind. She was too busy imagining herself handing over a smart leather folder crammed full of glossy photos of Edward Pym – aka Agent Kremlin– captured as he conducted clandestine meetings behind the conifers with sinister Russian spymasters. The dossier would include detailed lists of names and times and numerous close-ups of the Injured Hand. London Eye would smile in admiration. '*Excellent work, Seagull Three.*'

Now, she just had to work out how they were going to get close to Pym . . . She longed to make some notes – a plan of action, complete with bullet points and mind-maps – but London Eye was right, of course; it was essential not to leave a paper trail. She'd destroyed her notebook, as instructed, feeding the pages through the shredder in Dad's office. 'I'll just have to keep all my plans in my head,' she murmured to Drift. But he was fast asleep and dreaming of rock pools. Seconds later, Emily was asleep too – dreaming of codebooks and missing fingers.

Next morning the friends gathered to discuss their mission at the tree house in the old chestnut tree in the garden of Stone Cottage, hoisting Drift up with them in the basket pulley system they'd installed last summer.

'We should have guessed Pym was a villain,' Jack said, stretching out in the hammock. 'He's got a cat. Criminal masterminds *always* have cats in the films.' He pretended to stroke a large cat on his lap. 'Now, Mr Fibbles,' he cackled, 'we hatch another evil plot . . . '

Scott laughed. 'They're usually those fluffy white Persians though, not ordinary little tabbies. And, anyway, Pym looks more like a presenter from one of those boring gardening programmes on TV. *Remember, August is the perfect time to prune your cabbages . . .*' he droned.

'Stop messing around, you two!' Emily scolded, although she couldn't help grinning at Scott's TV gardener impression. 'Looking ordinary is exactly what he's trying to do! But this is serious. Kremlin could be a threat to national security. You heard what London Eye said about terrorist connections.'

Jack put on his serious face. Emily wasn't the only one who'd been thinking about the case. 'I've come up with an awesome plan for staking out Sunset Lodge,' he said. 'The ice-cream van is directly opposite, right? Obviously, we can't stand in the queue all day. So I've come up with a rota system. If we take our time choosing, I estimate that we can spin each visit out to twenty minutes – longer if there's a queue. So, to keep watch for, say, six hours, that's only eighteen trips in total. I don't mind taking the lion's share of the work. I can probably manage ten ice creams in that time, which means you two only need to eat four each!'

Jack paused to let his plan sink in.

Scott and Emily stared at him.

'I know!' Jack laughed. 'You're stunned by the sheer awesomeness of it!'

Scott shook his head very slowly. 'Firstly, I'm sure someone would notice if we spent the entire day at the ice-cream van – even if we took it in turns. Secondly, it'd cost a fortune in ice creams. Thirdly, you'd be sick!'

'Want to bet on it?' If he hadn't been stuck in the hammock Jack would have landed a swift kick on Scott's shin. 'You're just jealous *you* haven't come up with an idea.'

'That's where you're wrong!' Scott snapped. 'And my idea actually makes sense. We split up and keep watch from different positions. We'll be less noticeable if we're not in a group all the time.'

Emily stepped in before the brothers' argument turned into a wrestling bout. 'Let's combine both ideas. We'll split up. Jack's post can be the ice-cream van. Use your charm and make friends with Butterfly Girl and then you've got an excuse to hang around the van all day,' she told him.

'What charm?' Scott snorted.

'Ha ha!' Jack snapped. 'What am I supposed to talk to her about?'

'I dunno. What about butterflies?' Scott suggested. 'That's her thing.'

Emily jumped up and clapped her hands. 'Perfect! You can go the library and do some research first so you sound all knowledgeable.'

Jack flopped back in the hammock and groaned. He was willing to bet that if you looked in the *Guinness Book of World Records* for the Most Boring Activity Ever Invented, you'd find *going to the library to read about butterflies* right up there at Number One. 'Alright,' he mumbled reluctantly. 'And what are *you* going to do?'

Scott thought for a moment. 'I'll go to the bird hide and watch the house from the back.'

'Don't forget your flask of tea and your Digestives,' Jack joked, delighted that Scott would have almost as tedious a day as he would. He was starting to suspect that this whole espionage thing had been seriously over-rated in the movies!

Scott suddenly noticed that Emily had pulled a white smock out of her bag, pulled it over her head and pinned up her curls with a pair of paintbrushes. 'Er, is there something you want to share with the group?' he asked uncertainly.

Emily grinned. 'I'm an artist.'

'Of course you are,' Jack said, making a questioning face at Scott. Had yesterday's excitement sent Emily over the edge?

'That's my *legend*!' Emily said. 'I'm going to set up an easel on the seafront outside Sunset Lodge and paint. That way I can sit there all day and nobody will suspect a thing. I've borrowed a load of Mum's painting stuff.'

Scott frowned. 'Won't it seem a bit weird? There's all this beautiful scenery around and you're painting a shabby old house covered in scaffolding?'

Emily grinned. 'I thought of that!' She held up a box of watercolours and opened the lid with a flourish. 'Ta da!'

'*Paints,*' Jack said. 'So what?'

Emily sighed, but she was too pleased with her own handiwork to be annoyed for long. 'I've glued a mirror inside the lid. I can sit on the seafront, looking out over the beach and the sea, but I can watch what's going on behind me at Sunset Lodge at the same time.'

'Genius!' Scott and Jack exclaimed in stereo.

There were high-fives all round.

They couldn't wait to put their plan into action!

Eight

Stake-out

Two hours later Seagull One, Seagull Two and Seagull Three were in position.

Seagull One reported to the ice-cream van, ordered a ninety-nine and struck up a conversation with Butterfly Girl. It wasn't as difficult as he'd expected. As soon as he mentioned that he'd spotted a silver-studded blue near the old quarry that morning, it was plain sailing.

It was only half a fib; Jack *had* seen a silver-studded

blue that morning – at least, he'd seen a picture of one in *The Handbook of Cornish Butterflies,* while swotting up in the library.

'It's so great to meet another lepidoptery buff,' enthused Butterfly Girl – whose name, Jack now knew, was Josie. 'Most people think it's dead boring.'

'Lepi-what—' Jack started. Then he remembered: *lepidoptery* meant butterflies and moths. He was supposed to be an expert! *'Boring?'* he snorted. 'No way! Butterflies are cool.' He glanced across the road at Sunset Lodge. He wished Edward Pym would hurry up and appear. He wasn't sure how long he could keep up the witty lepidoptery banter.

Josie handed Jack an ice cream so immense that the cone was crumbling under the weight. 'On the house,' she said with a wink. 'Hey, maybe we could go out one day and you could show me those silver-studded blues?'

'Sorry, what?' Jack suddenly realized she'd asked him a question. Pym had finally emerged and was opening the gates onto the drive.

'Do you want to go out with me?' Josie repeated.

Jack nearly choked on his flake. Was she asking him on a date?

'I've heard there are some heath fritillaries about up near the quarry too,' Josie added.

Jack realized with relief that she was talking about butterfly hunting!

'Yeah, great,' Jack murmured vaguely, his eyes still

on Sunset Lodge. Pym was looking up and down the road now – waiting for his contact from the Russian secret service to arrive, no doubt!

'We could go this evening,' Josie was saying, 'when I finish my shift here.'

Jack took out his phone, trying to work out how to get a photo of Pym without looking like a stalker. Without knowing it, Josie helped him out. 'Good idea,' she laughed. 'Check your social diary!'

Jack took the cue and pretended to consult the appointments calendar on his phone. 'Yeah, that should be fine,' he murmured, all the while snapping pictures of Pym. Annoyingly, the man kept his hands thrust deep in his trouser pockets. *He's obviously hiding those missing fingers, Jack* thought.

'Let's say six o'clock?'

The little tabby cat scampered up to Pym and wound around his legs. Pym began to take his hands out of his pockets . . .

'Result!' Jack breathed.

Josie smiled. 'Good. I'm really looking forward to it.'

Pym scooped the little cat up in his arms. 'Oh, drat!' Jack muttered. Pym was wearing gardening gloves again!

Josie frowned. 'What's wrong? Can't you make that time?'

'Er, yeah, sure,' Jack said.

'It's a date then!'

Jack nodded, but he was watching a blue van pulling

into the drive at Sunset Lodge. Two men carrying hard hats climbed out. The older man, short and wiry, with a shaved head and droopy moustache, started unloading ladders and toolboxes from the back of the van. The younger guy, tall with fair curly hair, walked across the drive to talk to Pym. He stopped and turned to shout something to the other builder who had just dropped a box of spanners. They both roared with laughter.

It must have been a joke.

But Jack could only guess, because the men were speaking a foreign language.

Russian! Jack thought with a shiver of excitement.

Meanwhile, a little further along the seafront, Seagull Three had set up her stool and easel and sat facing out to sea. Drift curled up under the stool and went to sleep.

The customized paint box was angled so that Sunset Lodge was visible in the mirror. It was all working perfectly except for one unforeseen problem. Emily had attracted quite a crowd. Not only were the onlookers in danger of noticing that she was daubing random blobs of paint on the canvas; they were also blocking her view.

'Is that meant to be the ocean?' an elderly American man asked, tilting his head to one side.

'It's an abstract, expressionist seascape,' Emily told him, as if this were the most obvious fact in the world.

The man nodded wisely. 'Ah, yes, I'm seeing it now.'

Well I'm not, Emily thought crossly, glancing at her mirror. *You're standing in my way!* 'I'm sorry, but I can't work when I'm being watched,' she said.

The man shuffled away, herding the rest of the crowd with him.

Just in time for Emily to see the blue van arrive and the builders get out.

Emily noted the time and memorized the number plate. She heard the clatter of the spanners, the shouted joke and the laughter. And, like Jack, she thought the men were speaking Russian.

And Emily noticed something else as well: Pym was laughing and joining in the builders' joke. He could speak Russian too! She could tell he was a Russian agent a mile off!

Emily splodged a bit of yellow onto her canvas. It was supposed to be the sun, but looked more like an alien spaceship coming in to land. She chewed the end of her paintbrush. How was she going to get the concrete evidence that London Eye needed? It was impossible to get a photo of Kremlin's disfigured hand while he was wearing those gardening gloves. If she could get closer, perhaps she could record him talking in Russian to those 'builders' who were so obviously his minders.

Another glance in the mirror revealed that Kremlin – alias Edward Pym – had disappeared into the house. The fake builders were now on the scaffolding. Then suddenly Pym was wheeling a bike round from the side of the house. He was going out! Emily was about to follow when she saw him lean over the builders' van and slide a note under the windscreen wiper.

Emily was so excited she accidentally smudged red paint all over the sun.

That note had to be a coded message!

She looked along the seafront and noticed Seagull Two walking towards her. She caught his eye and gestured towards Pym with a tiny nod of her head. Scott gave an almost invisible thumbs-up to confirm that he would follow the target.

Now all Emily needed to do was get a look at that note. She glanced in her mirror. The tabby cat was chasing leaves on the drive near the van. That was it! She'd go and make a fuss of it. 'Stay close to me,' she told Drift. Then she strolled over the road to the end of the drive, where she crouched down and held out her hand. 'Come on, puss!' she coaxed.

The tabby eyed Emily and Drift warily and held its ground.

Emily shuffled closer. So far, so good. With Drift at her side there was no way the cat would come to her, so she would have to go to the cat – which was exactly what she wanted!

But suddenly the cat seemed to decide that Drift was harmless and began to trot towards Emily.

Oh, no, Emily thought. *Now I've got no excuse to*

creep nearer the van! 'Shoo!' she whispered. 'Go back up the drive! Look, there's a dog here!'

Drift was trying very hard to be good. He knew he wasn't allowed to chase cats, especially on stake-out duty, but that little tabby was challenging him to a game of tag. That superior flick of its whiskers meant only one thing: *Can't come and play because your owner won't let you? Poor little doggy!* Drift couldn't bear it any longer . . .

'Drift!' Emily shouted. 'Come ba—' But she stopped herself mid-call. Drift had chased the cat right under the van. 'No, don't come back, stay there!' she hissed, and she hurried up the drive after him. 'Just looking for my dog,' she called up to the men on the scaffolding. 'He's chased a cat under your van!' She did a mime of a dog and pointed at the van, just in case the Russian agents didn't speak much English. To her surprise, one of the builders, a tall black-haired guy with a ponytail poking out from under his hard hat, shouted down in a distinct Welsh accent.

'Right you are, love. Let us know if you need anything.'

Emily was taken aback for a moment. *But of course,* she reasoned. *Russian agents obviously have to speak fluent English so they can blend in!*

She checked over her shoulder to make sure the men were busy with their work again and peeked at the note.

Dwie nasady kominowe zostaną dostarczone w piątek

She was so excited she had to stop herself jumping up and down.

Instructions from Agent Kremlin to his minders. *In Russian!*

Emily slipped her phone from her bag and sneaked a photograph.

Then she called to Drift. He slunk out from under the van expecting a few stern words concerning cats' rights and self-discipline.

'Well done,' Emily laughed. 'Perfect timing!'

Drift twitched his spotted ear in puzzlement. He'd never understand humans as long as he lived!

'Just don't do it again,' Emily added, ruffling his ears just the way he liked.

—

Meanwhile Scott ran to the railing at the end of the beach where he'd left his bike, hopped on and pedalled after Pym. The old man headed across South Moor towards Castle Key village. As he followed some way behind, Scott mulled over his morning's observations.

He had headed to the bird hide and trained his binoculars on the back of Sunset Lodge. Nothing was happening and he couldn't see into the garden over the high fence. He was considering abandoning the mission when a delivery lorry had rumbled down the access track that ran between Sunset Lodge and Tamara Bradshaw's house next door. A small crane mounted on the back of the truck began to unload sacks and pallets of building supplies, swinging them round and dumping them into the back garden of Sunset Lodge in a clatter of whirring, grinding and clanging.

The height of the hoist meant that Scott could see exactly what was being unloaded, even over the high fence. There were all the usual building materials: bricks, wood, roof tiles, insulation foam . . . But then came some more *specialized* items: rolls of razor wire, a box of CCTV cameras, thick metal doors and a crate marked *Sure-Stop Glass.*

He planned to check it later, but Scott had a feeling he knew exactly what it was that Sure-Stop Glass was designed to stop!

Since when did retired gardeners need razor wire and *bulletproof glass*?

Surely it was a bit heavy duty for keeping the rabbits off the lettuces!

Scott had taken some pictures and hurried back to the seafront. That's when he'd noticed Pym leaving the house on his bike.

Now, up ahead, Pym was entering Castle Key village. He pedalled past the village hall and turned into Church Lane. Scott hung back near the graveyard and watched as the old man bent his back and wobbled with the effort of cycling up the steep hill – past Church Cottage, home of Colin Warnock the curate, past Lilac Cottage, home of Mrs Roberts the art teacher . . .

There was only one more house on Church Lane.

Scott could hardly believe his eyes.

Agent Kremlin was going to Stone Cottage!

Nine

The Gloved Hand

S cott leaped off his bike and hurtled up the garden
path. What did Edward Pym want with Aunt Kate?

Rudge's words were ringing in his ears: *He's an
extremely dangerous man!*

Scott's mind was seething with horrific images – Aunt
Kate being held at gunpoint, Aunt Kate with a knife
to her throat – when the front door opened and Pym
stepped out. Aunt Kate followed, smiling.

Scott dived backwards into a honeysuckle bush.

'Thank you for the crossword magazine,' Aunt Kate was saying.

'And thank *you*, Kate,' Pym replied. 'Those chocolate muffins were delicious!'

'See you at the meeting tonight.'

'I'll be there.' Pym turned and waved. He was wearing black lycra cycling gloves but there wasn't a gun or a knife to be seen. Moments later he was freewheeling back down Church Lane.

Scott waited a few minutes before going inside. Aunt Kate was in the living room, plumping cushions.

'Who was that man?' he asked ultra-casually.

'You mean Edward Pym?'

'What do you know about him?' Scott asked.

Aunt Kate reached up and gave Scott an affectionate hug as she passed on her way to the kitchen. 'You sound just like my father,' she laughed, 'the first time I went out courting when I was sixteen years old. *What do you know about that young man, Katherine?*' Aunt Kate put on a gruff voice. '*Is he from a respectable family?*'

Scott forced a laugh and followed her into the kitchen.

'If you must know, Edward has just moved to the island,' Aunt Kate told him. 'I met him in the library the other day. He's doing up one of those big houses near Westward Beach. He used to be the head gardener at a stately home in Yorkshire.' Aunt Kate grinned at Scott as she tied her apron round her waist. 'Is that enough background? Or should I hire a private investigator to check he's not an axe murderer?'

Scott followed her into the kitchen. He managed another laugh but it wasn't easy. If Rudge was right about Pym, *axe murderer* was the least of their worries! He sat down at the kitchen table. Glancing at the pile of newspapers he suddenly noticed a large beige envelope. The words G.C. MEETING were printed on it in an old-fashioned-typewriter font that made it look like something from a black and white war film.

Scott stared at the envelope. This was even worse than he'd thought! Edward Pym had said something about a meeting as he left. And didn't G.C. stand for *Government Communications*? Blood roared in his ears. He was starting to feel queasy. *Was Pym trying to drag Aunt Kate into his shady world of lies and subterfuge?*

Aunt Kate waved the wooden spoon she was drying in the direction of the envelope. 'Ah, there they are! My tickets for the Garden Club meeting tonight. We've got that celebrity gardener, Derek Hopkinson, talking to us about growing prize-winning dahlias. I asked Edward if he'd like to come along.' Aunt Kate took the envelope and popped it into her apron pocket. 'Now what would you and Jack like for dinner? I'll leave you something to eat while I'm out.'

Scott thought for a moment. 'Actually, could we come to the Garden Club meeting with you?'

Aunt Kate laughed. 'Since when were you boys interested in *dahlias*?'

Good question, Scott thought. He wasn't even sure what a dahlia *was* and he was probably letting himself in for the most mind-numbingly boring evening of his entire life. But it would be a chance to observe Pym at close quarters, to see what he wanted from Aunt Kate and maybe even to get a photo of that injured hand. 'Er, just thought it might be fun,' he said.

'Are you alright?' Aunt Kate asked. 'You've gone very pale.'

'I'm fine,' Scott replied weakly.

When the friends gathered in the tree house to compare notes that afternoon – taking the tin of leftover chocolate muffins with them – there was plenty to report.

Scott had the photos of bulletproof glass, razor wire and other security equipment being unloaded from the crane, and the worrying news about Pym's visit to Aunt Kate. Emily had her mysterious note from Pym to his 'builders'. She couldn't wait to get to work on trying to translate it.

And Jack had a date with Josie! 'We're going to look for butterflies,' he groaned.

'Hang on!' Scott protested. 'You can't go off with your girlfriend tonight. I've told Aunt Kate we'll go to the Garden Club meeting.'

Jack's mouth fell open. '*Garden Club?*' he echoed, as if Scott had signed them up for advanced belly dancing lessons. 'What did you do that for?'

'So we can keep an eye on Pym, course!'

'It's a great idea,' Emily agreed. 'I know! I'll use Jack's ticket and come to the Garden Club meeting with you. Jack can go out with Butterfly Girl.'

Jack grinned at Scott. 'Looks like everyone's got dates tonight then! You, me *and* Aunt Kate!'

Scott scrumpled a muffin case into a ball and fired it at his brother. 'I'm not going on a date. Emily's not like an actual *girl*.'

Emily aimed a muffin case at Scott. 'Thanks very much!' she laughed.

Jack clambered out of the hammock. 'I'd better get ready for butterfly spotting. Have fun with the dahlia brigade.' He paused halfway down the rope ladder and stuck his head up through the platform. 'This secret agent job isn't all it's cracked up to be in the films, is it? James Bond gets fast cars and explosives. How come we get butterflies and flowers?'

—

The village hall was already filling up when Emily and Scott slipped in at the back. A banner with the words **WINNING WITH DAHLIAS** had been draped above the stage, where a table had been set out with vases of brightly coloured pom-pom shaped flowers.

'I'm guessing those are dahlias?' Scott whispered to Emily.

'Sherlock Holmes would be jealous of your deductive powers!' Emily giggled. Suddenly her expression became deadly serious. She nudged Scott in the ribs and hissed, 'Kremlin at three o'clock.'

Scott was used to Emily's spy-speak. He turned to the right – where the three would be on a clock face – and saw Edward Pym standing near the refreshments table talking to Aunt Kate. He looked smart in a slightly crumpled way, in a cream linen suit and blue shirt. Aunt Kate offered him a cup of tea. Scott and Emily both tracked the cup as it moved towards Pym's hand, like a pair of hungry Labradors watching a bacon sandwich.

'Gloves!' they groaned in unison. 'Not again!'

Pym was wearing leather gloves with a pattern of little holes on the backs.

Camouflaged among the crowds of dahlia fanatics, Emily and Scott ventured closer to the table.

Pym was smiling at Aunt Kate. 'How did you get on with that crossword?'

Aunt Kate laughed. 'You were right. Three Down was a stinker of a clue . . .' Her answer was cut short by an old lady elbowing her way across the hall and launching herself at Edward Pym as if he were a bargain handbag in the January sales.

Castle Key's Number One Busybody had switched her usual orange high-visibility jacket and pink Disney Princess cycling helmet for a dress that looked like an explosion in a flower shop and a hat that was like something the Queen would wear to the wedding of a distant relative she'd never really liked. 'I'm Irene Loveday,' she fog-horned. 'My dahlias are generally acknowledged to be the best in Cornwall. Not that I'm one to Blow My Own Truncheon, of course, but I've won second prize in the flower show three years running.' She lowered her voice to a stage whisper. 'It *would* have been first prize if Diana White hadn't bribed the judges with her homemade fudge! Custard cream?' Mrs Loveday thrust a plate of biscuits under Pym's nose.

'Oh, er, no, thank you.' Pym turned back to Aunt Kate. 'But I'm sure you had no problem figuring out that clue!'

Mrs Loveday wasn't giving up that easily. Armed with a back-up plate of biscuits she regrouped for another assault. 'Chocolate finger?'

As Edward Pym shrank back from the incoming plate, tea slopped into his saucer and over his hand.

Mrs Loveday tugged at a leather finger. 'I'll dab that glove down in the Ladies for you. Ooh, I do like a man who wears driving gloves. Terribly Extinguished, I always think.'

Scott and Emily could hardly believe their luck; it was Pym's right hand! Mrs Loveday was going to be their secret weapon in unmasking Agent Kremlin! Emily reached for her phone, poised to take a photograph.

But Pym snatched his hand away. 'No!' he cried, so loudly that everyone turned to look. 'I'm sorry,' he said, quickly getting his voice back under control. 'But there's really no need to trouble yourself.'

Suddenly Mrs Loveday's attention was caught by a commotion near the door. 'That'll be Derek Hopkinson arriving,' she said. 'I *must* go and introduce myself.' With that, she shot off like a gossip-seeking missile.

Scott and Emily looked at each other, crushed by disappointment. Were they destined *never* to discover the secret of the gloved hand?

—

Meanwhile, Jack's 'date' was going well. Josie was full of funny stories about life at Carrickstowe Sixth Form, and she'd brought loads of sweets from the ice-cream van. Jack was bursting to tell her about Operation Skylark, but he remembered Rudge's instructions – *absolute secrecy* – and valiantly resisted the temptation.

'So, whereabouts did you see those silver-studded blues?' Josie asked, after they'd been wandering near the quarry for some time. Jack gazed around. Even if he *had* seen butterflies up here, how would you ever tell one bit of moor from another? He couldn't see what all the fuss was about anyway. If you had to go stalking around after wildlife, why not at least pick something exciting like a lion safari in Africa? In desperation he pointed at a random patch of heather.

As if by magic, a cloud of little blue butterflies fluttered up like a handful of petals flung into the air.

Josie was so excited she hugged him.

But that's when Jack's luck ran out . . .

While Josie crawled around taking photographs, he sat down. Almost immediately, he felt a stabbing pain in his bottom. He sprang to his feet and looked down.

A huge snake with black zig-zags down its back was slithering off into the bracken.

'Aggggh!' he screamed. 'I've been bitten by a black mamba!'

Josie glanced at the snake. 'It's an adder. Don't worry. It hurts a bit but it's not serious.'

'*Hurts a bit?*' Jack cried as he rolled around. 'I'm in mortal agony here! I could be paralyzed. I saw it on *The Planet's Deadliest Animals*! You have to suck the venom out!'

Josie looked horrified. Then she laughed. 'Hang on! What's that?' She pointed at the back of Jack's shorts. A large thistle was caught in the weave of the thin cotton fabric.

Jack stopped writhing and removed the thistle. The pain stopped.

Josie grinned. 'It's OK. I won't say a word!'

Ten

Cracking the Code

Next morning Emily unlocked the secret compartment in the desk in her bedroom and took out the printout she'd made of the note she'd found on the builders' van – she'd deleted the original photo from her phone for security reasons, of course.

She waited until her parents were busy in the guest lounge, then went down to the family living room, logged onto Dad's computer and searched the internet for a translation website. Carefully, she typed the words of the message – *Dwie nasady kominowe zostaną dostarczone w piątek* – into the box. Then she scrolled through the menu of languages, selected *Russian to English*, and waited with bated breath.

When the result popped up on the screen Emily was so excited she hardly dared look. This was going to prove beyond doubt that Pym was Agent Kremlin *and* reveal the nature of his current mission. Agent London Eye was going to be so impressed!

Error: Cannot translate.

'Error? What do you mean, *error*?' Emily snapped at the computer. She tried another website but that one refused to translate the message too. And so did the next. Emily's heart sank. Of course, Pym must have written the message in code! She gazed gloomily at the screen, wondering how to even start code-breaking a Russian message. Her eyes wandered over the long list of languages on the translation menu: Afrikaans, Albanian, Arabic . . .

Suddenly she remembered something Rudge had said: Kremlin was fluent in many languages. Maybe this note wasn't in Russian, but one of the other languages he spoke!

Fired by new hope, Emily typed the message in again and began to work her way through the alphabet of languages: Bulgarian, Catalan, Chinese, Croatian. The same message popped up again and again: *Error: Cannot translate.*

If this turns out to be Welsh or Zulu I could be here for a very long time, Emily thought. *Maybe it is code after all!* She was on the point of giving up when she clicked on Polish.

Emily stared at the screen. Then she looked away, rubbed her eyes and stared again. The words that now appeared in the translation box weren't *Error: Cannot translate* but the message was just as baffling: *Two chimney pots will be delivered on Friday.*

Emily translated it back to Polish and then to English again just to be sure.

She leaned back in the chair and closed her eyes.

She'd been braced for something momentous and shocking to do with terrorist cells or nuclear bombs, but what did Kremlin mean by *chimney pots*? It *had* to be spy jargon for secret documents or undercover agents or something. She ran up to her room and rifled through all her books on espionage, including *Survival Guide for Secret Agents.*

There was no mention of *chimney pots*. But whatever they were, they were coming on Friday and today was Monday.

She only had four days to find out.

Meanwhile, at Stone Cottage, Jack was reclining on the sofa watching cartoons while Scott played *Total Strategy*. It was the latest version of his favourite game and it ran at lightning speed on his new laptop – the one he'd bought with his share of the money from the sale of the antique bottles of brandy they'd found during Operation Compass - but he just couldn't concentrate on outwitting the zombies. He was too busy worrying about Aunt Kate. He gave up and paused the game. 'We've got to steer her away from getting too friendly with Pym.'

Jack glanced up from *The Simpsons* and shrugged. 'As long as she's not planning to run off with him, what's the problem?'

Scott sighed. 'You should have seen them together at that meeting. Aunt Kate must have been reading too many of those romantic novels she writes. *Tall silver-haired stranger rides into town and sweeps the lonely island girl off her feet . . .*'

Jack pretended to stick his fingers down his throat.

'We can't let her fall in love with an enemy agent,' Scott fretted, 'but we can't warn her either because we promised Rudge to keep the whole operation secret.'

'Why don't you just tell her that you saw Pym kissing Mrs Loveday?' Jack joked. 'That'd put her off! Or tell her he's got some hideous contagious disease like the Black Death!'

Scott was about to point out the numerous flaws in

Jack's suggestions when the doorbell rang. It was Emily and Drift. Scott could tell from Emily's face that she was dying to tell them something. She glanced around the living room as if checking for concealed bugging devices. 'Two chimney pots will be delivered on Friday!' she hissed.

Jack made a noise like an alarm going off. 'Wah-wah-wah! Psycho Girl on the loose. Please clear the building. I repeat, please clear the building.'

Emily batted him with a sofa cushion. 'That's the message that Kremlin left on the van. It's in Polish.'

'*Chimney pots?*' Scott echoed. 'What's Pym on about?'

Emily shrugged. 'I don't know. But he's obviously expecting an important consignment on Friday. At least it means we've got *something* to report to Rudge. We're supposed to leave him a message in the bird hide on North Moor by tonight, remember? He's MI5. He'll know what *chimney pot* means.'

'Well, you can count me out,' Jack muttered. 'I'm never going outside again. Nature keeps attacking me!'

Scott rolled his eyes. 'Don't ask! He *says* he was bitten by an adder.'

Emily winced. 'Ooh, nasty! OK, you stay and rest. Scott and I can leave the message in the bird hide.'

It didn't take long to agree on the message: *no sightings of hand yet but two chimney pots due on Friday.*

'That's the plain text,' Emily said. 'Now we have to hide it in another message that looks innocent using the number sequence that Rudge gave us.'

'Which is one-eight-two-five,' Scott remembered.

Emily nodded. 'That means the hidden message is made up by skipping one letter of the carrier sentence, then eight then two then five. Then you just keep repeating that pattern till you've concealed the whole message.'

Jack had no idea what Emily was talking about but he nodded wisely.

Emily took a scrap of paper and wrote . . .

N-O - - - - - - - - S - - I - - - - - G - H - - - - - -
- - T - - I - - - - - -N - G - - - - - - - - - S

'That's the first two words of the message we want to hide,' she explained. 'The letters are separated by blanks – one then eight then two then five. We have to fill those blanks in with other letters to make something that reads like a normal sentence.'

'Oh, I get it!' Scott took Emily's pen and started filling in the blanks. 'What about something like this?' he suggested. 'It needs to be something about birds that won't look out of place in the logbook in the hide.'

NO OTHER LARKS DOING SONGS.
HOWEVER, NOTED IT - - - - - N -G - - - -
- - - -S

'Brilliant!' Emily exclaimed. 'Now we just have to keep going and conceal the rest of the message like that.'

Jack left Emily and Scott to it and stretched out on the sofa again. After all, Emily had told him to get some rest; he was only obeying orders!

—

When Scott met Emily on the common that afternoon to cycle to the bird hide he was surprised to see that she was dressed like a miniature version of Rudge. She had the khaki shorts, the binoculars and camera and even the ankle socks and sandals. The outfit was completed by a white t-shirt with a picture of a blackbird.

'I know Rudge is your hero, Em, but don't you think that starting to *dress* like him is a bit over the top?'

'I'm not copying London Eye!' Emily protested. 'I'm dressing like a birdwatcher so that it'll be less suspicious if anyone sees me going into the bird hide.'

Soon they were pedalling along the bumpy track past the old tin mine. The stone walls of the ruined engine house and chimney stack glowed in the sunshine, and bees buzzed in the golden gorse. Scott and Drift kept watch with the bikes while Emily cut across the moor on foot to the bird hide. She glanced around to make sure no one was about, then slipped inside. She opened the logbook at the latest page, wrote in the date and carefully copied down the sentence with its hidden message in small neat handwriting.

Then she pushed open the door to leave.

She heard the crunch of a foot on dry bracken.

Her heart tried to jump out through her mouth. Had Kremlin or one of his henchmen followed her to the hide?

Emily looked up to see Josie from the ice-cream van waving to her. 'Hi! You're Jack's friend, aren't you?'

But Emily shook her head. 'I'm sorry, you must have mistaken me for someone else.' She bolted back to Scott and Drift, her thoughts in a tailspin.

Was it just a coincidence that Josie was hanging around near the tin mine today?

Or was she working with Kremlin?

Eleven

Walking into Trouble

Jack almost fell out of the hammock. 'Of course I didn't tell Josie about Operation Skylark!'

The friends were in the tree house the following morning.

'So Butterfly Girl just *happened* to be wandering around the *exact* spot where we left the message for Rudge?' Scott asked.

'She must be working with Kremlin,' Emily put in.

'Rubbish!' Jack spluttered. 'You two are paranoid. She was just looking for butterflies!' It was so unfair. He hadn't breathed a word to Josie, but he might as well have gone round the whole island shouting about Operation Skylark with a megaphone since nobody believed him anyway.

Scott began climbing down the rope ladder. 'We'll have to go back to Westward Beach and keep watch on Josie, as well as Pym.' He fell silent as he reached the ground. Aunt Kate was coming into the garden to peg washing on the line.

'Did I hear you say you're going to Westward Beach?' Aunt Kate asked. 'Could you take something to Edward Pym's house for me?' She hurried back into the kitchen and reappeared with a Royal Wedding cake tin. 'I've just made another batch of chocolate muffins. He enjoyed them so much the other day.'

Scott stared at William and Kate smiling up at him from the lid of the tin. *No contact with the target.* That was one of Rudge's ground rules. But how were they going to deliver muffins without *contact*? Not to mention that Aunt Kate was getting even friendlier with Pym. Sending him cakes when it wasn't even his birthday!

'Well, don't all volunteer at once,' Aunt Kate laughed.

Scott felt a stab of guilt. Aunt Kate was always so kind and had never once complained about their scrapes and misadventures; he couldn't bear her to think they were too ungrateful to run an errand. 'Of course we will,' he said.

'*No contact!*' Emily hissed, once Aunt Kate was out of hearing.

Scott shrugged. 'I know, but . . .'

'What's the problem?' Jack asked. 'We can just leave the tin at the end of the drive and scarper.' He selected a muffin and took a bite. 'What?' he asked, seeing the others gaping at him. 'Doesn't the delivery boy get a tip?'

As they cycled across South Moor Emily felt as if there were eyes everywhere, watching from behind gorse bushes and under rocks. Every rabbit-rustle in the bracken made her jump.

What if Josie had intercepted the message in the bird hide and reported to Kremlin? A man who dealt with terrorists and nuclear missiles for a living wasn't exactly going to say tut-tut and send them on their way! And now they were risking blowing their cover to deliver a tin of muffins!

A reconnaissance mission along the seafront revealed that the big iron gates were open at Sunset Lodge.

Drilling and banging noises were coming from the back of the house.

'All clear,' Emily whispered.

Hardly breaking his stride, Scott set the tin down near the gatepost as gingerly as if it were packed with high explosives rather than chocolate muffins.

They were about to make their getaway when the little tabby cat slunk out from the shadows and pounced on Drift's tail.

Drift yipped in surprise.

Edward Pym stepped out from behind the hedge. He was carrying a chainsaw.

For a split second he froze and glanced from side to side, his steely blue eyes narrowed like a soldier's on full alert. Then he stooped to stroke the cat. 'This little chap was a stray but he sort of adopted me when I moved in,' he said. 'I've named him Boomerang because he keeps coming back. I've grown quite fond of him.'

Emily couldn't help admiring Kremlin, even though he was an enemy agent. His nice-old-man act was *very* convincing.

Pym smiled as he straightened up. 'Now, how can I help you?'

There was nothing for it but to tell the truth. Scott picked up the cake tin and held it out. 'These are for you. From our great-aunt.'

Pym took the tin. 'Ah, so you must be Scott? And Jack? And your friend, Emily? Kate told me all about you.' He pulled the gardening glove from his left hand and shook hands all round.

As no-contact situations go, Scott thought, *this isn't exactly running to plan.*

'Wait here a moment,' Pym said. 'I'll give you a thank you note for your aunt. I've got a picture for her too!'

'Love letter, more like!' Jack muttered as Pym disappeared into the house. 'Do we *look* like postmen?'

As they waited, Scott, Jack, Emily and Drift gradually sidled further up the drive until they were almost at the front porch. With its pillars and turrets and fancy carvings, Sunset Lodge must once have been imposing, but now it had the ramshackle look of a haunted house in a fairground. In contrast, Emily noticed, a state-of-the-art security system had been installed next to the door. There was a keypad, a videophone and something that looked like an iris recognition device. CCTV cameras had been mounted under the porch roof too. Kremlin obviously didn't welcome uninvited visitors!

Jack couldn't resist pressing his eye to the iris reader. He jumped back as the door opened and Pym reappeared, holding a large white envelope. At the same moment, one of the builders – the guy with the ponytail and the Welsh accent – came hurtling round the side of the house from the back. 'Come quickly!' he yelled. 'Jan's drilled through a water pipe!'

Edward Pym rushed away with the builder.

The friends looked at the open door and then at each other.

'Time for a quick recce?' Jack said.

'No!' Emily whispered, tugging him back by the t-shirt, even though she was itching to see inside the house too. 'There are cameras.'

Scott pointed at the cables hanging from the wall. 'They're not connected yet.'

'Well, what are we waiting for then?' Jack said. 'He's practically *invited* us to come in and have a look around.'

Scott wished he'd kept quiet. 'I'm not sure ...'

But Jack was already inside. Reluctantly, Scott followed.

A tight knot in the pit of her stomach told Emily that they were walking into trouble, but it was just too tempting to resist. 'Come on, Drift,' she whispered.

They tiptoed along a corridor of paint-spattered floorboards, brushing their fingers over crumbling plaster and tatters of old wallpaper and peeping into rooms as they passed. One was empty except for a grand piano. Others contained stepladders and pots of paint or old furniture stacked to the ceiling.

At the end of the corridor Jack pushed open a heavy oak door. At last, a room that was lived in! It had been done out to look like the library of a wealthy Victorian gentleman. There were polished wooden desks and bookshelves stuffed with leather-bound volumes. Sherlock Holmes and Dr Watson would have felt at home sitting in the button-backed leather armchairs at either side of the fireplace – although, Scott thought, they might have been a bit baffled by the two computers on the desk.

The friends began to scout around for evidence that Pym really was Agent Kremlin, but the desk was empty, the filing cabinets were all locked and the computers were powered down and had plastic security strips all over them, so that Pym could tell if anyone tampered with them while he wasn't there.

Scott was beginning to despair of finding anything useful when he brushed against a laptop computer open on the arm of one of the leather chairs. It beeped and the screen flickered on. That was odd. Why wasn't this computer secure like the others? He glanced at the screen, which was now displaying a black and white photo and the print menu. This must be the picture Pym had printed out for Aunt Kate, Scott figured. Pym had obviously not bothered to shut the laptop down when he came back to the door, thinking he'd only be a moment.

Scott knelt to take a closer look at the photograph. Could it be true? It was Aunt Kate!

But this wasn't the old lady Aunt Kate of today.

In the picture she was young and blonde and very beautiful. She was standing with a group of people in evening dress, holding a champagne glass. There were flower arrangements in the background and a sign saying *Moscow Ballroom*. Suddenly something else caught Scott's eye. The dark-haired man in the tuxedo standing next to her, looking like an old-fashioned film star at an awards ceremony – it was Edward Pym!

Scott's stomach lurched with fear. Was Aunt Kate an enemy agent too?

No, of course not, he told himself. *Get a grip!* Aunt Kate had travelled a lot in her youth. She'd obviously just been invited to a grand party and had no idea that the handsome young man she was talking to was a Russian spy!

But why did Pym want Aunt Kate to have the picture?

In one swift move, Scott reached into his pocket, took out an old memory stick he'd been carrying around for days, inserted it into the laptop and clicked *Directory Copy.* He hadn't really expected it to work. Surely there were all kinds of passwords in place? But Pym must have left himself logged in when he came to the door. No doubt the laptop would shut down automatically after a few minutes, but for now it was letting Scott copy the files.

Scott jumped at a sudden noise behind him. He spun round to see Jack doing a backwards ninja-leap away from the bookcase, which appeared to be in the process of turning like a revolving door! An entire wall of communications equipment rotated into view, stuffed with headphones, satellite dishes, listening devices and radio jammers. At the same time the surface of the desk flipped over to reveal a control panel crammed with more dials and flashing lights than a DJ's mixing desk. A flat screen and an aerial were also sliding up out of the desktop. A metal shutter rolled down over the window.

Startled by the furniture coming to life, Emily accidentally pulled the top off the gold ink pen she'd picked up. A dart shot out of the end, whizzed past Scott's ear and embedded itself in the painting of a bowl of fruit above the mantelpiece.

Drift whimpered and sprang into Emily's arms.

Scott glared at Jack. 'What have you *done*?'

'Nothing!' Jack spluttered. 'I just touched one of the books!'

'Quick!' Emily urged. 'We've got to put all this stuff back and get out before Kremlin comes back. If he finds us snooping around in here . . .'

She didn't need to finish the sentence.

The friends flew around the room frantically trying to put everything in order. Jack tried to shove the screen and the aerial back into the desk, but they kept popping up again. Scott snatched his memory stick from the laptop, then tried to push the bookcase back into place. Emily pulled the dart from the painting.

Jack kicked the desk. 'Aggh! This is hopeless.'

That's when they heard footsteps in the corridor outside.

Twelve

Trapped!

Fear scuttled down Emily's backbone like a spider. Kremlin was right outside the door now. They had to find another way out. But the window was still blocked off by the metal shutter and there were no other doors. Emily ran and stuck her head into the fireplace, but the chimney was far too narrow for escape.

Speechless with panic, Jack pointed at the gap

between the side of the bookcase-slash-equipment-rack and the wall.

'We'll have to try it,' Scott said, pulling Emily by the hand and bundling her through the gap. She grabbed Drift's collar just in time and dragged him with her. Behind her Jack was making desperate *mmpph* noises. He was stuck! Emily grabbed his arm and heaved until he catapulted through the gap after her. Scott, who had been shoving from the other side, staggered through in his wake and they all tumbled against a damp brick wall at the back of a chamber barely big enough for the four of them to stand up in.

Emily thought her heart was about to turn inside out with terror. The bookcase was now completely closed behind them. Had they just shut themselves into their own dungeon? But then she felt Drift's cold nose butting against her knee. He was scrabbling at the wall with his paws. She crouched down and felt a blast of cold air. Could this be a way out? Hardly daring to hope, she took her torch from her bag and shone it down to reveal a square window in the brickwork. Inside was a metal construction like a rusty old slide from a long-forgotten play park.

'It's some kind of chute,' Scott whispered, peering over her shoulder. 'Must have been for coal for the fire or something. It's our only way out.'

'You mean we have to climb up this thing?' Jack asked.

'You have a better idea?' Scott hissed.

Somehow, by wedging their knees against the sides, they were able to pull themselves up the chute, shuffling Drift along between them. It was excruciating work. By the time they reached the top Emily thought her arm muscles would burst into flames. But at last they emerged into an old storeroom, full of copper cooking pots and jars of ancient pickled vegetables.

They crept out into a passageway. Running footsteps echoed around the house.

'Kremlin's still looking for us,' Emily gasped. 'Let's get out of here!'

The friends ran along corridors, up and down stairs and through empty rooms, but every window was locked and none of the doors led to the outside world. They came out on a landing at the top of a flight of stairs and heard footsteps and voices coming up the stairs behind them.

Three doors led off the landing. Jack picked the middle one at random and pulled Scott and Emily through the door with him. Drift ran in at their heels.

The huge room was steeped in shadow, its windows all boarded up. As Jack scanned the room for somewhere to hide, he took in decaying plasterwork, a broken chandelier hanging drunkenly from the ceiling and a grandfather clock with shattered glass. Chairs and sofas and sideboards had all been draped with white dustsheets; they loomed out of the gloom like the ghosts of ancient furniture. Jack ran to a sofa and dived under the sheet. Emily and Drift piled in next to him. Scott rolled under a table.

Jack held his breath. He heard the squeak of the door handle, the groan of the hinges and the creak of footsteps on the floorboards. This was torture. His nose was squashed against a musty old velvet cushion. On top of that his arm was twisted under Emily's foot and Drift was breathing dog-breath in his face. He didn't know how much longer he could keep up the pretence of being a sofa cushion.

The footsteps creaked further into the room. 'I'm sure I heard someone come in here.' The voice belonged to Edward Pym.

Jack gulped. The gulp turned into a splutter and – he just couldn't keep it in any longer – the splutter turned into a cough.

He closed his eyes and braced himself for the worst.

'There's something on that sofa!' Jack recognized the voice as belonging to the Welsh builder.

Crushed against Jack's side, Emily peeped out from under the dustsheet. She had to bite back a scream. Pym was holding a gold pen just like the one she'd picked up in the office, and he was pointing it at the sofa. He was going to fire what looked like tranquilizer darts at them! She knew she had only one card left to play.

'Distraction!' she whispered to Drift. It might not

work but at least it would give Drift the chance to run to safety.

Pym aimed the pen. Emily felt the air sing as the arrow sped towards her.

Drift shot out from the sofa. *Distraction* was his all-time favourite command. He just had to find something really *naughty* and then do it! And this time he knew exactly what his Naughty Thing was going to be! He'd been picking up whiffs of feline smugness all round the house. And he could see the twitch of a tabby tail taunting him from the doorway.

There was a joyful bark, an indignant meow and a skittering of claws as Drift and Boomerang hightailed it out of the room.

'It's just that dog!' The builder laughed. 'It's the one those kids had with them. It must have chased your cat into the house. It chased it under the van the other day too.'

'Ah, that explains it!' Pym sounded very relieved. He began walking back towards the door. 'Boomerang must have fled through my office and somehow triggered all the mechanisms. Well, I'd better go and see whether that pipe's fixed yet.'

Scott made himself count to twenty to be sure the two men had left before throwing off the sheet. 'Phew! That was a close one,' he breathed. 'Now, let's get out of here while Pym's in the back garden.'

Emily clutched his arm. 'Wait! I think that dart hit Jack.'

'Yeah, it did!' Jack grumbled from the sofa. 'I felt it. Right there!' He pointed to the seat of his shorts. 'Have I got a bullseye pinned to my butt or something? Splinters, thistles, er, I mean *adders*, and now tranquilizer darts!'

'So how come you're not *tranquilized* then?' Scott asked.

Jack shrugged. 'Must be my awesome inner strength.'

'Or,' Scott suggested, pulling the dart out of the arm of the sofa and holding it up, 'it *could* be the fact that it only grazed you on the way past.'

Emily laughed with relief and headed for the door, where she found Drift waiting for her. She hugged him and buried her face in his fur.

Drift had saved the day once again!

Thirteen

Rendezvous at Willow Island

At last the friends found the front door and sneaked out of Sunset Lodge.

Dizzy with freedom they raced down the drive and on to the beach. They didn't stop running until they were on the promontory near the viewpoint. They flopped down among the rocks, panting and laughing. Jack felt the springy grass against his back and the sun on his face. He gazed up at the seagulls circling in the

111

stained-glass blue sky and listened to the waves crashing against the rocks far below. He ran his finger over the hole in the fabric of his shorts leg. The dart had gone right through, missing him by a fraction of a millimetre!

'What about that office?' he laughed. 'If that doesn't prove Pym's a Russian spy, I'll kiss Mrs Loveday!' Jack put on a gravelly film voiceover voice. 'By day it's an ordinary office,' he intoned, 'but as darkness falls it morphs into the top-secret headquarters of the evil Agent Kremlin . . .' He switched back to his usual voice. 'Of course, if I hadn't brilliantly figured out which book to pull from the bookcase, we wouldn't have known about it!'

Scott rolled his eyes. 'You mean we wouldn't almost have been caught red-handed.' He rubbed his arms. 'And we wouldn't have needed to crawl up that chute. I feel as if my biceps have been through a blender.'

'Me too,' Emily groaned. 'But I managed to get a few pictures of all those gadgets.' She sat up and showed the boys the photos on her phone. Suddenly a worrying thought clouded her excitement. 'What's Pym going to do when he realizes we've gone without waiting for the thank you note for Aunt Kate?'

Scott thought for a moment. 'With any luck he'll just assume that we gave up waiting for him and went home – once Drift had come back from his cat-chasing mission, of course.' He stroked Drift's ears.

Drift looked up and wagged his tail happily.

Boomerang had been a great sport; he'd let Drift chase him all round the house before he'd taken refuge on top of a wardrobe.

Jack got up and wandered over to the viewpoint pillar, idly reading the names of the far-flung places on the compass: Casablanca, the London Eye, the Great Wall of China. He replayed the escape from Sunset Lodge in his mind. He promoted himself to the lead role, adding a few extra scenes in which he heroically fought off Pym and his posse of henchmen with his bare hands. Of course, in reality there was only one henchman. That Welsh 'builder' had to be a Russian secret agent working with Kremlin, otherwise he'd have been outside fixing the pipes with the others. It was odd that Pym and his sidekick kept speaking English and not Russian when they were on their own together, though . . .

Jack's thoughts were interrupted by his brother joining him at the pillar. Scott raked his hands through his hair. 'I saw something dead weird in that office,' he said.

Emily jumped to her feet. 'What?' she asked.

Scott described the old photograph of Aunt Kate and Edward Pym and held up the memory stick. 'I made a copy of it.'

Emily's dark eyes opened so wide she looked like a startled owl. 'The picture was taken in *Moscow*? That's in Russia! You don't think Aunt Kate was working with Kremlin, do you?'

'I'm sure Aunt Kate would never betray her country,' Scott said quickly. Even so he couldn't help wondering why Aunt Kate had kept quiet about having met Pym before. Suddenly, a terrible thought came to him. 'What if Pym's trying to *blackmail* Aunt Kate? You know, threaten to report her as a Russian spy unless she coughs up a huge payment. He wants Aunt Kate to see that photo so she'll know he's got evidence to prove his story.' As he spoke he realized it could be something even worse than money. 'Maybe he's blackmailing Aunt Kate into doing a hazardous mission for him – like planting a bomb or stealing military secrets or something! We've got to warn her.'

Emily frowned. She was worried about Aunt Kate too, but they'd promised Rudge they wouldn't tell *anyone*. 'Let's arrange another meeting with London Eye first,' she suggested. 'With all the evidence we've got from inside Sunset Lodge, surely he'll have enough to convince his boss to swoop in and arrest Pym immediately. Then he won't be able to do anything, let alone blackmail Aunt Kate.'

Scott nodded thoughtfully. 'OK. And with luck we'll have some more evidence on here too.' He waved the memory stick. 'I didn't *only* copy the photo of Aunt Kate from Pym's laptop. I copied the whole directory – at least, as many files as there was time for, before we had to get out of the office.'

Emily gasped with excitement. 'Wow! That's brilliant!

I bet there's loads of stuff on there that proves Pym's an enemy agent.'

Scott slid the memory stick back in his pocket. 'Let's get back to Stone Cottage. I can't wait to open these files and see what we've got.'

Jack grinned. 'What are we waiting for?'

'Race you to the bikes!' Emily laughed, already haring down the slope.

After a high-speed cycle ride back to Castle Key, Scott raced up to the attic bedroom he shared with Jack, switched on his laptop and inserted the memory stick. In addition to the photograph, only three other files had copied successfully in the few seconds the device had been connected to Pym's laptop. *Never mind*, Scott thought. *We only need one set of instructions from his contacts in Russia or one diagram of a top-secret military base . . .* but, to his disappointment, the only diagram was of the electrical circuits at Sunset Lodge. The other two files were a bill for paving slabs and a boring letter from the council about water rates.

Scott trudged to the tree house to break the bad news to the other two.

'So, that's our brilliant evidence?' Jack snorted. 'I can't see Rudge being very impressed with a letter from the council. We'll be thrown out of spy school for this!'

Emily sighed with frustration but she tried to look on the bright side. 'Of course,' she said. 'It makes sense. Any decent agent would keep all his sensitive files on those high-security computers we saw in the office. That laptop was obviously just Pym's personal computer.' Suddenly she brightened. 'And we do have something else we can take to Rudge. I almost forgot – I saw Pym's right hand!'

Scott and Jack both turned and gaped at her. 'And you didn't mention this before, because . . .' Jack said.

'There was so much going on! It was when we were hiding. I peeped out from under the dustsheet as Pym was about to fire the dart-pen. He didn't have his gloves on.'

'Are you *trying* to kill us with suspense?' Scott groaned. 'What did it look like?'

'I only got a glimpse,' Emily admitted. 'It was sort of red and mangled, but I couldn't see if there were any missing fingers. I know it's not photographic evidence, but at least we can tell Rudge I saw it with my own eyes.'

Jack and Scott agreed. 'OK,' Scott said. 'We'll leave another message in the bird hide saying we want a rendezvous first thing tomorrow morning. We need to set up a good meeting place.'

'What about Willow Island in the middle of Polhallow Lake?' Emily suggested. 'There's a kayak moored on the jetty near Polhallow Cottage that Rudge can use.'

'Good idea,' Jack said. Paddling out to the tiny island would be fun!

Together they worked out the details of the message and encoded it using their one-eight-two-five key again. 'I'll take the message to the bird hide this time,' Scott offered, when they'd finally finished. 'On one condition.'

'What?' Emily asked.

'That I don't have to dress up as a birdwatcher! I've *never* worn socks and sandals in my life and I don't plan to start now!'

That evening Scott observed Aunt Kate closely, looking for signs that she was either (a) a Russian spy working with Kremlin or (b) an innocent victim of a blackmail campaign. But as she served up chicken pie followed by strawberry trifle she showed no sign of harbouring any dark secrets.

After dinner, Scott hurried upstairs to his bedroom and opened up the Moscow ballroom photograph on his laptop again. He stared at the young woman with the blonde curls and the champagne glass. Maybe he'd been getting worked up over nothing and this was just a woman who *looked* like Aunt Kate. But then he noticed that someone had written in the names at the bottom of the photograph in small white writing, and there was no doubting it any more.

Katherine Trelawney. That was Aunt Kate's name! Scott's eyes flicked to the man standing beside her.

Was he about to discover Edward Pym's real identity?

But the name had been scratched out. 'Why am I not surprised?' Scott murmured.

Scott sighed. Oh, well. There was nothing else he could do now. He closed the photo file and clicked onto *Total Strategy,* looking forward to completing a couple more levels, but to his frustration the game refused to start up.

He picked up his book instead. Then he threw it down again. It was one of the old Dirk Hazard spy novels from Aunt Kate's shelf, and Scott had had enough of spies for one day!

—

The friends arrived early for their meeting with Rudge the following morning.

They'd arranged to borrow kayaks from the little boathouse that belonged to friends of Emily's parents, and were soon paddling towards the island, droplets flying from their paddles, sparkling in the bright morning sunlight like fairy lights. Drift sat on Emily's knees in the cockpit of her kayak, eagerly watching the waterbirds using the mirror-smooth surface of the lake as a runway.

The island was deserted apart from ducks, wild geese and a stately grey heron fishing in the shallows. Scott,

Jack and Emily pulled the boats up onto the tiny beach and arranged them into a Y shape; they'd told Rudge in their coded message that this would be the signal to show it was safe for him to join them. The bright red and yellow kayaks would be clearly visible from the window of Polhallow Cottage.

They settled down to wait under cover of the trailing fronds of the giant willow tree that gave the island its name. Emily trained her binoculars on the little whitewashed cottage on the north shore of the lake. She was surprised to see a kayak already halfway to the island from the jetty near Polhallow Cottage. Soon it was close enough to hear the splash of the paddles.

Emily couldn't wait to discuss the intelligence-gathering mission with Agent London Eye. 'Did you get our first message?' she asked, before Rudge was even out of the kayak. He nodded as he dragged the boat onto dry land.

'Good,' Emily said. 'So, you'll know that I translated the message that Kremlin planted on the builders' van: *two chimney pots to be delivered on Friday.*'

A bemused expression flickered across Rudge's face. He looked even paler and weedier than before, Jack thought. His diet of tortilla chips and instant noodles couldn't be doing him much good.

'Obviously *chimney pots* is code for something else,' Emily pressed on. 'Does it refer to weapons or documents or . . .'

Rudge shook his head. 'I'm afraid I'm not at liberty to reveal that information.'

Emily's face fell.

Rudge sat down with his back against the willow trunk, listening as the friends recounted the incident at Sunset Lodge and showed him pictures of the gadgets in Pym's office.

Finally, Emily revealed her prize information. 'I saw his right hand. It's definitely injured.'

Rudge started to look interested. 'Have you got a photograph?'

'Well, no,' Emily mumbled. 'I only caught a glimpse.'

Rudge sighed. 'You shouldn't have gone inside the house. Maybe getting you kids involved has been a mistake.'

Emily swallowed, fighting back tears. This wasn't turning out at all how she'd pictured her report to Agent London Eye. No shiny brown leather dossier full of photos. No 'Excellent work, Seagull Three'. She couldn't bear it if her first official mission for MI5 ended in failure. 'Just give us a bit longer,' she pleaded. 'We'll get the photo.'

'Alright,' Rudge grunted. 'You've got twenty-four hours.'

'We'd better not meet here again, had we?' Emily suggested, cheering up a bit now there was a new plan to work on. 'How about the standing stones on North Moor. It's not far. Same time tomorrow?'

Rudge gave a brusque nod. He got up and brushed dry leaves off his jeans. 'By the way,' he said to Scott as he began to slide the kayak back into the water, 'What was in the files you copied from Pym's laptop?'

'Oh, nothing,' Scott said quickly. He hadn't planned to lie. But he didn't want to mention Aunt Kate's connection with Pym if he could help it, in case MI5 got the wrong idea and started investigating her. 'I couldn't open them.'

'Are you sure?' Rudge asked suspiciously. 'Let me have the memory stick. I'll be able to open the files.'

'I, er, haven't got it with me,' Scott mumbled. That part was true, at least. He'd hidden it in his sock drawer. 'I'll bring it next time.' *After I've deleted the picture of Aunt Kate*, he thought.

Rudge nodded. 'Make sure you do. There could be vital information in those files.'

As they watched Rudge paddle away, Scott frowned. Something was bothering him. It wasn't only the thought of having a twenty-four hour deadline to photograph the Hand of Doom (as Jack had started calling it), or even that he'd just lied to an MI5 intelligence officer. It was that feeling you get when you've just chipped a tooth and your tongue keeps going back to the rough bit. Somewhere, somehow, something didn't quite fit.

Fourteen

Making it Up

By the time they'd stowed the kayaks and cycled back to Castle Key, Jack was on a new mission of his own: Operation Enormous Fried Breakfast.

Luckily, Scott and Emily wanted in on the mission, and they were soon sitting in the window of Dotty's Tea Rooms tucking into sausages, eggs and bacon. As Jack doused his plate in ketchup he gazed out to the harbour, where Old Bob and the other fishermen were already landing their morning catches. 'So,' he said, when the sausages had kick-started his brain again, 'How are we going to get a photo of the Hand of Doom in the next . . .' he leaned over and looked at Emily's watch . . . 'twenty-two and a half hours?'

Scott glanced around to check there was nobody close enough to hear them. 'First of all we've got to get him to take his gloves off.'

Emily remained silent. *Odd*, Jack thought. He wouldn't call Emily *bossy* – not if there was any danger she might hear him – but she didn't usually miss a chance to tell them exactly what they should be doing. This time, though, she was sitting with her elbows on the table, staring at a slice of toast as if it held the meaning of life. 'Something wrong with that toast?' he asked.

'It's not the toast,' Emily murmured, passing it under the table to Drift. 'It's Rudge.'

'Don't worry, Em,' Scott said kindly. 'We'll think of a way to get the evidence. And if we don't, it's not like we're officially working for MI5. He can't fire us!'

'That's just the point,' Emily sighed.

Jack and Scott leaned across the table. Emily's voice was so quiet that they had to lip-read her words. 'I don't think *Rudge* is working for MI5 either.'

Jack grinned. 'Just because he wouldn't tell you what *chimney pots* means?'

'I'm serious,' Emily sighed. 'I've been thinking about it ever since we left Willow Island. He's just not following protocols. Remember how quickly he kayaked to meet us? Unless he's Superman he must have started out *before* we signalled that it was safe . . .'

'Maybe he was just impatient?' Scott suggested.

Emily shook her head. 'And he didn't do a sweep to make sure there were no listening devices around, or tell me to delete the photos of Pym's office from my phone, or . . .'

'But if he's not MI5, how come he knows all about codenames and stuff?' Jack interrupted.

'But does he though? We came up with the idea of leaving a coded message in the bird hide and the meeting places and the safety signals. He's just gone along with it all.' Emily pushed away her plate and slumped over the table with her head on her arms. The sickening feeling that she'd been duped was welling up inside her like food poisoning. She'd been so thrilled about helping with a real, live undercover operation that she'd overlooked the fact that a genuine MI5 agent wouldn't disclose his mission to random strangers without first running detailed background checks! 'I think he's been lying to us all along,' she groaned.

They all fell silent for a moment as a couple of backpackers came into the café and asked Dotty for directions to Land's End. 'We're doing all the sights in Europe,' one of them said in an Australian accent. 'The Leaning Tower of Pisa, Buckingham Palace, the Eiffel Tower . . . We've travelled thousands of miles!'

As the backpackers left, Jack's knife and fork suddenly clattered to the table. An image had flashed into his mind: Rudge talking about Edward Pym as he stood hunched over the pillar at the viewpoint *with its list of distances to famous places around the world.* Jack knew from *extensive* experience that when you were making up a story off the top of your head, you usually just looked around you for inspiration (to this day, his history teacher believed that Jack owned a pair of homework-eating puppies called Pencil and Sharpener.) 'Emily's right! Rudge was making all those agent names up as he went along!'

Scott stared at him across the table. 'And how do you know that?'

Jack grinned. '*Kremlin, London Eye . . .* Think about it! He was reading the place names off that compass thingy on the pillar. It just came to me when I heard those backpackers talking about all the landmarks they'd visited.'

Scott slapped his palm to his forehead. 'Of course! Rudge also said that one of Pym's identities was a German businessman called Dieter Eiffel. I thought it was a funny name. He must have made it up from seeing the sign to the *Eiffel Tower*!'

Emily nodded slowly. 'And he said Pym's hand was injured in Casablanca. That was on the compass too. It's a famous city in Morocco.' She paused. 'It *could* be a coincidence that all these names are on the compass . . .'

Scott looked up from tapping on the keyboard of his phone. He shook his head. 'I don't think so. I just checked the distance from here to the Kremlin. It's a famous building in Moscow. It's *one* thousand *eight* hundred and *twenty-five* miles.'

Jack made a blank face. 'What is this? The General Knowledge round?'

But Emily knew what Scott was getting at. 'One-eight-two-five was the sequence Rudge gave us for encoding the message. He read that off the compass as well!'

Scott nodded. 'I can't believe we didn't notice. He must be brilliant at reading upside-down.'

'He is,' Jack laughed grimly. 'Remember how he read *Ice-cream spy* in Emily's notebook when he first talked to us on Westward Beach?'

The three friends were silent for a long moment, all doing their best to digest the brain-boggling realization: Rudge wasn't an MI5 agent. Which meant Pym almost certainly wasn't Kremlin either.

'And yet . . .' Emily muttered, 'there must be *some* truth in Rudge's story. We know Pym *is* a Russian agent. We've seen the proof. Normal people don't have iris recognition devices on their doors and bulletproof glass and morphing offices and tranquilizer darts. And they don't write strange notes in Polish.'

'Or have old photos of Aunt Kate in Moscow on their computers,' Scott added.

Jack shrugged. 'Perhaps Rudge and Pym are *both* Russian spies. They could be in rival teams.'

'Spying's not like the Premier League or something,' Scott snorted. Suddenly his laughter died away. Mention of the photo of Aunt Kate had reminded him of that chipped-tooth feeling he'd had on Willow Island and he'd just worked out why. The answer sent a glacier-cold wave of fear through him. 'I think Rudge is spying on *us*,' he whispered.

Emily gasped. 'What do you mean?'

'He asked what was on the files I copied from Pym's laptop.' Scott paused and swallowed hard. 'But how did he *know* I'd copied any files? *We didn't tell him!*'

Jack almost choked on his Coke. He looked nervously over his shoulder as if expecting to see Rudge lurking behind him.

Emily took a deep breath and tried to think, even though her stomach was churning. 'Before we do any more surveillance on Pym we need to find out what Rudge is up to.'

Before they left the café, the friends had a plan. They would meet Rudge at the standing stones as planned the next morning. Or rather, Emily and Jack would meet him. Scott, meanwhile, would go for a snoop in Polhallow Cottage to find out more about the mysterious MI5 agent who wasn't.

'One minor problem,' Jack pointed out. 'How will

you get in? I don't suppose Rudge leaves the key under the mat.'

Scott groaned. He hadn't thought of that. And he wasn't sure he wanted to end up with a criminal record for breaking and entering!

But Emily rummaged in her bag, pulled out one of her old notebooks and flicked to the back page. 'Ah, yes, I thought so,' she murmured. 'It's Thursday tomorrow. Mrs Loveday does the cleaning and laundry at Polhallow Cottage on Thursday mornings. You could sneak in while she's there.'

Jack grinned. He'd always suspected that Emily had drawn up a spreadsheet to keep track of everyone's movements on the island. Now he knew it was true!

—

Early the next morning, Scott stationed himself behind an oak tree close to Polhallow Cottage. He watched Rudge drive off for his meeting at the standing stones. Five minutes later, Mrs Loveday came pedalling along the lane. She propped her bike against the wall, pulled a jailer-sized bunch of keys from the pocket of her high-visibility jacket and opened the door. She began carrying mops and brooms from her bike trailer into the house, singing along loudly to Michael Jackson on her iPod as she worked.

Scott crept to the cottage and peered through the

kitchen window. Plates were piled up in the sink and tortilla chip packets and crushed beer cans were strewn across the table. Mrs Loveday planted her hands on her hips and tutted at the mess. Then she set to work.

At last she lugged the vacuum cleaner upstairs and Scott saw his chance. He eased open the door and tiptoed inside. He soon realized he needn't have bothered with the easing and tiptoeing part; what with Michael Jackson and the hoovering, he could've marched into the cottage with a brass band.

Scott made for the kitchen. There was a leather jacket slung over the back of a chair, but there were no ID cards or notebooks in the pockets. A sports bag on the floor contained only a few pairs of socks. He moved to Rudge's laptop on the table. Normally, he wouldn't go poking his nose into someone else's computer, but since Rudge had clearly been doing a lot of nose-poking of his own lately, Scott felt he deserved a quick peek.

But Scott couldn't even get a blank screen up without reams of passwords and PIN numbers. He was on the point of giving up when he noticed a sheet of paper on the printer next to the laptop. It was a list of computer files and websites. At the top was www.chelseafc.com. Scott couldn't help smiling. Chelsea was *his* team too. Surely Rudge couldn't be *all* bad if he was a Chelsea supporter! The next site was *Total Strategy Hints and Tips*. It looked like Rudge was into the same kind of computer games too! But gradually Scott realized that *all* the filenames and websites on the list were familiar: the guitar store where he'd ordered some sheet music yesterday, his favourite YouTube clips . . .

Then he saw something that made the hairs stand up on the back of his neck.

It was the Facebook fan page he'd set up for his band, The Banners. How did Rudge even know about The Banners? They were pretty good, if Scott said so himself, but he'd be the first to admit that they weren't exactly world-famous.

Last night Scott had added some photos from their end-of-term school gig.

This was a complete list of *everything* he'd done on his laptop for the last two days.

Scott's knees turned to marshmallow. He gripped the edge of the table for support.

No wonder Rudge knows I copied files from Pym's computer, Scott thought. *Somehow he can see inside my laptop!*

Fifteen

Breaking and Exiting

Meanwhile Jack, Emily and Drift were at the standing stones. Drift was having a wonderful time following delicious vole and rabbit scents around the three huge ancient stones that leaned together as if whispering secrets to each other beneath the mighty capstone.

Emily and Jack, on the other hand, were not having so much fun. They were trying to keep Rudge talking to give Scott as long as possible in Polhallow Cottage.

Things were not going well.

'I don't know why I'm wasting my time with this,' Rudge grumbled, wiping his forehead with a grubby handkerchief. The heat, which had been building all week, had reached stifling levels this morning.

Emily repeated their story. 'We took some pictures but they didn't come out very well.' She waved her phone under Rudge's nose. She and Jack had staged some photographs earlier – Jack had daubed red paint on his fingers and jiggled them around, so that the pictures showed a blurry shape that just *might* have been a maimed hand.

'These pictures are useless!' Rudge snapped. 'And where's your mate with that memory stick? I want to know what he's up to, secretly copying files!'

Jack and Emily looked at each other, racking their brains for a cover story for Scott, but Rudge wasn't waiting around for explanations. He made a gesture with his hands like a conductor cutting off the last note of an orchestra. 'That's it! You kids need to remember that none of this ever happened.'

'We could have another try. Can't you tell us a bit more about Kremlin?' Jack asked, playing for time.

'No. I. Can. Not.' Rudge pronounced the words as if each one began with a capital letter. 'And if MI5 get wind that you've been leaking information, they, I mean *we*, will take it extremely seriously. Do I make myself clear?'

Jack and Emily nodded solemnly. 'Perfectly,' Jack muttered.

Rudge marched off towards his car. Emily ran after him. 'What will you do next?'

'That's classified information.' Rudge folded himself into the driver's seat, slammed the door and revved the engine.

Emily and Jack watched as he roared off down the track towards the road.

'We were right,' Jack said. 'He's not MI5. He said *they* not *we*.'

Emily nodded slowly. 'I'll warn Scott that he's coming back.' She took out her phone and stared at the screen in disbelief. *No service!* She tried again but with no success. 'It must be interference from the coming storm!'

'What storm?' Jack asked.

'Look!' Emily shouted, pointing at the blue-black clouds swelling like enormous bruises above the western horizon.

'Oh, yeah!' Jack plucked his damp t-shirt from his chest. 'I thought it was getting a bit muggy.' Suddenly he realized Scott was in deep trouble. The mood Rudge was in, if he caught him in Polhallow Cottage he'd probably shoot first, ask questions later. 'What are we going to do?' he gulped.

'Run!' Emily yelled, grabbing Jack by the arm. 'If

we head due south cross-country we might get there in time. Rudge has to go the long way round by road in the car.' She glanced over her shoulder. 'Come on, Drift!'

Jack ran after Emily, leaping tussocks of grass, dodging gorse bushes, scrambling over rocks. It was like doing one of those army assault courses, except in a sauna. Leg muscles aching, lungs burning, only the thought of Scott being used for target practice kept him going.

'There's the cottage!' Emily puffed.

Jack looked down a long heathery slope to see the little white building on the lake shore below.

'And there's Rudge!' Jack gasped, pointing to the black car speeding along the track like a turbo-charged beetle. 'He's almost there!'

—

Meanwhile Scott was still gazing dumbfounded at his computer's life story.

Suddenly he heard a noise.

Startled out of his trance, Scott dived under the table, his heart galloping like a buffalo stampede.

Rudge was back already!

Why hadn't Jack and Emily phoned to warn him?

Ker-thunk, ker-thunk, ker-thunk.

Relief surged through Scott's veins. It was only the

vacuum cleaner being bounced down the stairs!

He heard the front door open and close, the key turn in the lock, and the crunch of Mrs Loveday's bike wheels on the gravel as she cycled away. He crawled out from under the table and was taking a photo of the printout when he heard another sound.

A car was pulling up outside. Scott stole to the window and peeped out from behind the curtain.

Rudge was nosing the Toyota into the parking space at the side of the cottage.

Scott ran to the door and reached for the thumb-latch. That's when he realized that Mrs Loveday had locked him in! Panicking now, he cast about for another way out.

He heard the key turn in the door. There was no time to lose. He tried the window above the table but it was locked.

The front door was opening. He was going to be caught.

Suddenly Scott heard barking.

And not just *any* barking – huge frenzied explosions of over-the-top howling and growling.

Rudge was inside the cottage now, but he was pinned to the spot by Drift's Bark Attack. 'Get off! Blasted animal!' he yelled.

Scott knew he only had moments before Rudge saw him. He spotted a small window above the sink in the kitchen. He ran over, climbed up and forced it open. He squeezed his head and shoulders through and pushed off from the hot tap with his feet. With a final desperate wriggle he shot out and landed upside-down in a tub of marigolds on the patio.

Was Breaking and Exiting *a criminal offence?* he wondered, as he scrambled out of the tub and fled across the moor.

—

Jack aimed the remote. He'd been through the channels a hundred times. It didn't take long. Aunt Kate's prehistoric black and white telly only picked up five channels and there was nothing good on any of them. After the excitement of the morning's marathon run across the moors, and Scott's narrow escape from Polhallow Cottage (aided by Drift's valiant Bark Attack), the evening was turning out to be a bit boring.

Scott was huddled over his laptop trying to figure out how Rudge had got a list of his computer activities. Jack had to admit that that was spooky, but Scott had totally freaked out about it. He'd spent hours updating his virus checkers and stressing about internet security.

Emily was curled up in an armchair with Drift, working her way through every book they had in the library about MI5, MI6 and MI-Anything-Else looking for information that might shed light on the mysterious *chimney pots* message.

Jack helped himself to a medicinal jam tart. Aunt Kate had made them before she popped out to visit Mrs Roberts next door at Lilac Cottage. He began flicking through the pages of *Extreme Butterflies*. Josie had brought it round for him to borrow. *Wow,* he thought, *those Queen Alexandra Birdwings really are monsters. Wingspan up to thirty centimetres!*

Suddenly Jack was jolted out of imagining a butterfly the size of a pigeon by Scott yelling 'Aha! I should have noticed this before when *Total Strategy* wouldn't start up the other night.'

'Noticed what?' Jack asked.

'*Total Strategy* does an on-line licence check when you start it up. The reason it couldn't complete the check is that there's a spyware virus already using the same network address on my computer to send information to some suspicious-looking internet site,' Scott explained. 'Rudge must be downloading the information from that address. I just wish I knew how he'd got this spyware onto my laptop in the first place. I never download stuff from the internet that I'm not totally sure about, so it must have been from a memory stick or . . .'

The phone rang in the hall.

'I'll go!' Jack shouted, glad of an excuse to escape Scott's lecture on computer security.

'Who was that?' Scott asked when Jack returned to the living room.

Jack cleared his throat and waited for Emily to look up. He had a feeling she'd want to hear this too.

'That,' he said, 'was Edward Pym!'

Sixteen

Shock Tactics

'Edward Pym?' Scott and Emily chorused.

The History of MI5 dropped from Emily's hands and slid to the floor. 'Oh, no!' she gasped. 'Does he know we've been spying on him?'

'Did he warn us to keep away?' Scott asked. 'Did he make any threats?'

Jack held up his hands to ward off the questions. 'Actually, it was Aunt Kate he wanted.'

Emily sighed with relief. 'Another crossword or something?'

Jack grinned. 'I think those two have moved on from crosswords, if you know what I mean! The message was "Thank your great-aunt for the invitation to join her for a picnic on Westward Beach tonight".'

'*Picnic?*' Emily echoed.

'*Tonight?*' Scott gulped.

Jack nodded. 'Pym says he'll bring the champagne and strawberries!'

'Champagne?'

'*Strawberries?*' Scott sank his head into his hands. 'This is worse than I thought. They've gone all *romantic*.'

'Oh, no,' Jack groaned. 'If they get married, Aunt Kate might not want us to come and stay any more.'

'It's not that!' Scott snapped. 'We can't let Aunt Kate go off having lovey-dovey picnics with a dangerous Russian agent. He could talk her into blowing up Buckingham Palace or something. She'd be on the run for the rest of her life.'

Jack hugged a cushion to his chest. 'And then we'd *never* get to come and stay at Stone Cottage again.'

'We have to tell her,' Emily said solemnly.

'You're right,' Scott agreed. 'But we'll have to break it to her gently. I think she really likes him.'

Emily moved her books to one side and started making plans. 'We'll make sure she's sitting down. And have some hot tea with tons of sugar ready in case she goes into shock. And we'd better have a blanket on standby. It says in *Surivival Tips for Secret Agents* that warmth is of paramount importance for a shock reaction.'

'I could put her in the recovery position!' Jack offered.

Scott checked his watch. 'She should be back any minute. I'll start on the tea.'

Scott rehearsed his lines as he waited for the kettle to boil. *Aunt Kate, I'm afraid we've got bad news . . .* no, that sounded as if someone had died. *Aunt Kate, we need to talk about your relationship with Pym . . .* no, that was even worse, like something from the problem page in a teen magazine . . . *Aunt Kate, this man's going to break your heart . . .* no, that just sounded like a Country and Western song . . .

He almost dropped the milk jug as he heard Aunt Kate bustle in through the front door. She paused at the hall mirror and adjusted her hairgrips. She waved to Scott in the kitchen, before continuing into the living room where she greeted Emily and Jack with a cheerful hello.

Oh, dear, Scott thought. *Aunt Kate seems so happy these days.* They were going to have to handle this *extremely* delicately . . .

Scott loaded a tray with the teapot, a large mug and the sugar bowl and hurried into the living room. Aunt Kate was sitting in her favourite armchair. Emily was hovering behind her with the quilt off Jack's bed in her arms. Scott set down the tray on the coffee table and took a deep breath. *Here goes . . .*

But before he could say a word Jack beat him to it. 'Your new boyfriend's a spy!' he blurted.

Scott and Emily glared at Jack. So much for breaking it gently!

'Boyfriend?' Aunt Kate spluttered. 'A *spy*?'

'Yeah, a Russian one,' Jack said. 'With tranquilizer darts and terrorist connections.'

'A *Russian* spy?' Aunt Kate rocked back in her chair. She looked as if she was going to burst out laughing.

Hysterical with shock, Scott thought, exchanging a glance with Emily. He began spooning sugar into the mug. Emily threw the quilt over Aunt Kate's shoulders.

'What are you doing?' Aunt Kate laughed, shrugging off the quilt. 'It's sweltering in here!'

'You need it,' Emily said in a soothing voice. 'You're in shock.'

'What I *need*,' Aunt Kate said firmly, 'is for you three to explain what you're talking about. I take it the "boyfriend" you're referring to is Edward Pym?'

Scott nodded and handed her the tea.

'Now what makes you so sure Edward's a Russian spy?'

Between them Scott, Jack and Emily explained about the bulletproof glass and the iris recognition device and the revolving bookcase and the hand that was injured in an explosion in Casablanca in 1992.

'Why were you snooping around Edward's house in the first place?' Aunt Kate asked, wincing as she took a sip of super-sweet tea.

'Oh, er, Drift was chasing this cat,' Emily said quickly. It was the truth. Just not exactly the whole truth.

Scott held up his laptop and showed Aunt Kate the photograph. 'There's this as well,' he said in a grim voice. 'I think Pym is planning to blackmail you.'

Aunt Kate laughed. 'Heavens! I've not seen that photo for years. Is this what gave you the idea he's my boyfriend? The fact that I once met him at a party?'

Jack grinned. 'Well, that and the fact that he just phoned to confirm the details of your date tonight.'

'Date?' Aunt Kate laughed. 'What date?'

'The romantic picnic on Westward Beach this evening?' Emily prompted.

'Picnic!' Aunt Kate exclaimed. 'Why on earth would I want to go for a picnic on the beach this evening? There's a storm about to break.' She shook her head. 'You've let your imaginations run away with you. Edward Pym is just a nice ordinary man and he's *not* my boyfriend. I don't think you should say any more about this spy nonsense. People might get the wrong idea.' Aunt Kate smiled and got up to go to the kitchen, taking the empty jam tart plate with her. But as she reached the doorway she turned round. 'Just a moment! What did you say about Edward Pym's hand?'

'It was injured in an explosion in Casablanca in 1992,' Jack repeated helpfully.

All of a sudden Aunt Kate was speaking in a low, quavering voice that Scott had never heard before. 'Who told you about his hand? I take it you didn't invent that story yourselves?'

'A man called Rudge,' Scott said, fear trickling through his stomach. Somehow the conversation had crossed a line – like one of those arguments that starts out as a joke until someone pushes it too far. 'He's pretending to be a birdwatcher, but he told us he was from MI5.'

'He was lying,' Emily said bitterly.

Still gripping the jam tart plate, Aunt Kate sank back into her chair. 'This is a very serious matter. Tell me everything this man knows – or *thinks* he knows – about Edward Pym.'

Scott, Emily and Jack looked at each other. They were all frightened now.

Scott gulped. 'I think he knows *everything*. I've just figured out that he must have installed some kind of spy software on Pym's computer. It's the only way it could have got onto my computer as well. The virus downloaded itself onto my memory stick from Pym's laptop and then transferred to *my* laptop. It's like there's an invisible spy inside Pym's computer – and now in mine as well – sending copies of everything to Rudge.'

'So, how come Rudge was so keen for you to give him your memory stick if he already knew the contents of all the files you copied?' Emily asked.

Scott shrugged. 'I guess he just wanted to find out what I was up to. He knew I'd copied those files but hadn't told him about it . . .'

Aunt Kate sprang up from her chair. The jam tart plate fell to the floor and shattered. Pastry crumbs scattered across the carpet but she didn't notice. 'Take my word for it,' she said. 'Edward Pym is *not* a Russian spy, but this *is* a matter of national security. I have to go and make some calls.'

And with that she was gone.

Seventeen

Meeting at Sunset

Emily and the boys stared in silence at the door through which Aunt Kate had disappeared. They stared at the broken plate. Then they stared at each other.

Drift's ears drooped. All this silent staring was making his fur stand on end.

But suddenly they all began talking at once.

'What did she mean, *national security*?' Jack demanded.

'How does she know Pym's not a Russian spy?' Scott added.

Emily knelt and began clearing up the pieces of broken china. She tried to make sense of Aunt Kate's reaction – and of everything that had happened since they'd first embarked on Operation Skylark. It was clear that Rudge was not who he'd claimed to be. For some reason he'd hacked into Pym's computer. But if Pym wasn't a Russian agent, who exactly was he? One thing Emily was sure of; there was more to Pym than a retired gardener who had a thing about crosswords and chocolate muffins. Suddenly she thought of another big question. 'If *Aunt Kate* didn't invite Pym for a picnic on the beach tonight, *who did*?'

'Rudge!' the boys whispered in unison.

Emily nodded. 'He must've forged a note from Aunt Kate to lure Pym into meeting him on the beach tonight. But why?'

Jack shrugged. 'No idea. But I bet *he's* not bringing champers and strawberries.'

'I have a bad feeling about this,' Scott said.

Emily dumped the pieces of plate on the coffee table. If Pym came to any harm it would be all her fault. She was the one who'd persuaded the boys to start helping Rudge in the first place. 'That's it! We've got to warn Pym against going on that "date"!'

'There should be a record of his number on the phone from when he called,' Scott said, running into the hall.

But he came back a moment later. 'The number's not coming up. Pym must be ex-directory. Not surprising, I suppose, since he seems to have a secret identity.'

'In that case,' Emily said, already heading for the door. 'We'll just have to go to Sunset Lodge and warn him in person.'

—

The friends cycled across South Moor at top speed. There was no time to lose. They didn't know what time Pym thought he was meeting Aunt Kate but it was already well into the evening.

The sun was beginning to set in a luminous orange sky mottled with swollen black thunderclouds. The electric charge of the approaching storm fizzed in the air, like the smell of a burnt-out fuse. By the time they reached Sunset Lodge fat raindrops were plopping onto the drive, making dark circles the size of saucers.

The gates were open but when the friends hammered on the door there was no reply.

'He must have left already,' Emily groaned.

They trailed back down the drive. As they came out onto the seafront Scott turned to Jack. 'Did Pym say on the phone exactly where he and Aunt Kate were planning to meet? Westward Beach is huge.'

'I can't remember.' Jack replayed the call in his head. *On the beach . . . a nice walk . . .* He gazed along the seafront in search of inspiration. In the distance the derelict pier was silhouetted against the technicolour sky, looking spookier than ever. That was it! The pier! 'Yes!' he cried, punching the air. 'Pym said they were going for a walk along the little harbour beyond the old pier.'

They tore along the seafront to the pier and ducked down behind an outcrop of barnacle-encrusted rocks. From there they had a view of the tiny harbour below. It was little more than a slipway, a few mooring rings and an old wooden jetty. Tangled netting and discarded lobster pots were piled here and there. A handful of small fishing boats bobbed on the waves, which were starting to swell and break as the storm picked up.

'There he is!' Scott hissed.

Edward Pym was standing at the edge of the harbour looking out to sea. Raindrops had dappled the shoulders of his light linen suit. He was carrying a wicker picnic basket over his arm.

'No gloves!' Scott whispered.

Emily had noted that already. But, annoyingly, only Pym's left hand – the one carrying the basket – was visible. The other remained stubbornly hidden in his jacket pocket.

'Let's go and tell him that Aunt Kate isn't coming before Rudge turns up!' Jack whispered. 'What are we waiting for?'

For once Scott agreed. But as they were about to leave the cover of the rocks a dark figure emerged from the shadows under the pier. The tall man, dressed from head to foot in black – black trainers, black combat trousers and t-shirt and black woollen cap – clearly didn't want to be seen. He took three steps towards Pym and called out a name. 'Leonard Makepiece!'

Who's Leonard Makepiece? Emily wondered.

But Pym seemed to recognize the name. He spun round and came face to face with the man in black, who was now only metres behind him.

Time seemed to stand still.

The light of the setting sun broke through the thunderclouds, lighting up the edges like smouldering paper in a fireplace. The shaft of light flared over the man in black's pale features, painting them a grotesque shade of orange. And it glinted on an object in his outstretched hand.

'Put your hands on your head!' he ordered.

The man in black was Rudge. And he was holding a gun!

Edward Pym – Emily couldn't think of him as Leonard Makepiece even if that *was* his name – slowly set the basket on the ground and placed his hands on his thick white hair, his right hand concealed under his left. 'Can I help you?' he asked mildly, as if Rudge had simply stopped to ask the time.

Crouching behind the rocks the friends could barely

hear his words above the howl of the wind and the roar of the ocean.

Rudge's face twisted into an ugly sneer. 'I've arranged to meet some *friends* here,' he bellowed. 'I think they'll be very interested to make your acquaintance.'

Jack shuddered. There was something about the way Rudge lingered on the word *friends* that told him these weren't some old school chums he'd hooked up with on Facebook. These were the kind of friends that made enemies seem like a good idea.

Rudge pointed out to sea with a twitch of the gun. Pym's eyes shifted to look. Jack, Scott and Emily followed his gaze. A fishing boat was approaching the harbour, see-sawing over the turbulent waters, lit up as if on fire by the red light of the sinking sun.

'If you don't mind, I'd rather not,' Pym replied. 'I have another appointment to keep.'

Rudge sniggered. 'I think your lady friend has stood you up!'

Then he fired the gun.

Eighteen

Nowhere to Run

The crack of the gunshot rang round the harbour.

Emily forced herself to open her eyes and peek out from the rocks. She pictured the lifeless body lying on the ground, blood blossoming across the cream linen jacket.

But to her surprise Pym was still standing.

Rudge had missed at point blank range.

Either he's an atrocious shot, Emily thought, *or these*

'friends' want to meet Pym alive rather than dead.

But one thing was certain. If Rudge *did* mean to shoot Pym, there was no way he could miss a second time from *that* distance. They had to do something fast! Emily looked around for a way to create a diversion. She couldn't send Drift out into the fray this time, not when there were guns involved.

Rudge took a step towards Pym. As he put his foot down he stumbled on a low kerb. He had stepped onto the bottom of the slipway – the concrete ramp used for sliding boats down to the sea. And the top of the slipway, Emily now noticed, was right next to the rocks where they were hiding. An idea began to take shape. If only she had something to roll down that ramp . . .

She cast around and spotted a massive wooden post propped against the rocks. It looked as if it had once been part of a pillar holding up the pier. It was furred with green algae, one end as ragged as an old toothbrush, the other charred as if someone had tried using it for a beach bonfire.

'Help me!' Emily whispered to Scott and Jack, pointing from the post to the ramp and then to Rudge.

The old lump of timber was waterlogged and much heavier than Emily had imagined, but somehow they shifted it and pitched it onto the ramp, where it landed with a resounding thud. Rudge and Pym both spun round at the sound. Rudge watched open-mouthed as the post rattled towards him.

But at the very last second – just as Rudge was about to be bowled over like a skittle – he jumped aside and the post rolled past him into the sea. Pym made a lunge for Rudge, but Rudge dodged and turned the gun on him once again.

At that moment Drift sprang out from behind the rocks. Spooked by the earlier gunshot, he'd forgotten all his Undercover Surveillance Training and now some primitive canine instinct had taken over. All he knew was that a giant stick had just rolled down the slipway and he had to chase it.

'Not that blasted dog again!' Rudge yelled as Drift hurtled towards him.

'Drift!' Emily shouted. 'Come back!' She darted out from behind the rocks and began to run down the harbour. She'd forgotten her Undercover Surveillance Training too. All she cared about was getting Drift away from a man with a gun.

'No!' Jack bellowed, running after Emily.

Scott couldn't believe it. They were going to get themselves shot! But he had no choice but to run after them and try to get them all to safety somehow. He darted out just in time to see Drift fly past Rudge. Rudge staggered back and teetered perilously close to the edge of the harbour.

Another gunshot rang out.

Emily screamed. 'No-o-o-o! Drift!'

Scott felt a scream rising in his chest too, but then he

saw Drift bolting away towards the pier. Rudge hadn't hit him! He must have fired the gun by accident when Drift tipped him off balance. But he'd got his footing again now and was looking around. There was no time to lose. 'This way!' Scott yelled, catching up with Emily and Jack, grabbing their arms and diving for cover under the pier. He glanced back to see Pym not far behind them, followed by Rudge.

Jack landed face first in a heap of putrid seaweed. He sat up, spitting out globs of slime and pulling the clinging strands from his face.

Next to him Emily was crushing Drift to her chest. 'Never ever do that again!' She was sobbing and laughing at the same time, relief and love and anger all tumbling out together.

But Scott was already pulling them to their feet. 'Come on! No time for big reunions!'

'That's right!' Edward Pym panted as he joined them. 'I don't know what you kids are up to but we all need to get out of here. That idiot might actually hit something next time!'

Together they ran through the shadowy netherworld below the pier, ducking to avoid the rotten planks hanging from above, and dodging the fallen posts, rusty ironwork and other debris that had piled up beneath the derelict structure. Suddenly, they came to a halt, blocked by a wall that had collapsed under its own weight and fallen through the decking. A sign bearing the words BINGO HALL in faded red letters dangled from warped metal brackets.

They could hear Rudge, cursing as he blundered after them through the obstacle course.

It's like a scene from Total Strategy, Scott thought. But he'd take a horde of computer-generated zombie werewolves over one very real man with a gun any day. He spotted a flight of ramshackle wooden steps, as steep and narrow as a ladder. 'Up here!' he urged the others. He began to climb then turned back to help Emily carry Drift up the steps. At last they all tumbled out onto the top of the pier.

'When Rudge comes up the stairs we ambush him and wrangle the gun off him,' Scott shouted over the wailing wind, which lashed their faces with sand and rain and sea spray.

Pym nodded. They were still looking down into the stairwell, poised for attack, when they were startled by the sound of footsteps. Scott whipped round to see Rudge jogging along the pier towards them, still brandishing the gun. He must have found another way up!

Scott pulled Emily and Jack with him and they ran for their lives.

The decking was slippery and peppered with holes where floorboards had fallen through. Scott could feel the rotten wood giving way beneath his feet like wet sponge, but he kept running, past a rickety bandstand covered in graffiti, past a mountain of broken deckchairs, all swathed in long twisted shadows cast by the dying rays of the sun.

Finally they stumbled into the burnt-out shell of a building. A flock of starlings roosting among the crumbling rafters took fright. They protested raucously and rose in a vast black cloud.

Jack's heart was still racing from the shock of the starling flight when he bumped into a life-sized clown dummy. Its garishly painted face leered at him out of the shadows. He shrank away, only to come face to face with a grinning mechanical monkey clutching a pair of cymbals in its threadbare paws.

'It looks like an old amusement arcade,' Scott called as he ran.

A fortune-teller automaton with a cracked black wooden face and a tattered purple turban lurched forward out of a shattered glass booth. There was a whirr of clockwork and its hand shot out as if begging for money.

A pair of Punch and Judy puppets danced a macabre waltz as Emily brushed past.

Jack thought his heart would burst with terror. This freak show was scarier than his worst-ever nightmare.

'I can predict your future . . .' The fortune-teller's jaw clacked up and down in time to the robotic voice.

So can I! Jack thought. *I'm getting out of this place.*

'Run!' he yelled to the others.

But when they fled out of the door at the far end of the arcade there was nowhere left to run. They were at the end of the pier. There was a narrow stretch of decaying boardwalk, a broken guardrail and then nothing but dark storm-tossed waves as far as the eye could see.

Rudge had them cornered. He walked slowly towards them, the gun in his hand and a triumphant smile on his pale face.

Emily backed as close as she dared to the edge of the pier.

Pym, on the other hand, lounged against the railing, his right hand in his jacket pocket, looking as if he'd popped out for an evening stroll. 'Why don't you just tell me who you're working for?' he demanded coolly.

Rudge threw back his head with a high, reedy laugh. 'I'm not working *for* anyone. Viktor Kozlov has put a price on your head. *For the safe delivery of Leonard Makepiece, alias Agent Enigma, one million dollars.* And I'm going to claim every last cent of it.' He grinned at Jack, Scott and Emily. 'Thanks to a little help from my friends here!'

Viktor Kozlov? Agent Enigma? Emily's mind burned with questions. 'We're *not* his friends!' she protested.

'He told us he was MI5,' Scott said.

'And he said *you* were a Russian spy,' Jack added.

Pym laughed. 'MI5? He can't even shoot straight! And the only Russians around here are those goons.' He waved his left hand in the direction of the fishing boat which was close enough now for the whine of the motor to fill the brief lulls when the wind stopped to catch its breath.

There were two men in black waterproofs on the bow. It was clear they weren't fishermen – unless they were trying to shoot the mackerel out of the water with the machine guns they wore slung over their backs.

'Who are they?' Emily shouted.

'Ex-KGB henchmen, if I'm not mistaken,' Pym said. He looked back at Rudge. 'I take it you've arranged for them to deliver me to Kozlov.'

Rudge nodded smugly.

'In that case, I'd be most obliged if you'd let the kids – and the dog – go free first.' Pym still sounded as calm and polite as if requesting a table by the window in a posh restaurant.

Rudge shook his head. 'There's no way I can let these kids go. They know far too much.'

Jack gulped. Rudge was waving the gun around again. Was he going to line them up and shoot them like a one-man firing squad? Jack wasn't ready to die! It would be such a waste when there were still five weeks of summer holidays ahead . . .

Pym sighed as if Rudge had disappointed him by serving a badly cooked steak. 'You're not going to *shoot* them?'

Rudge sneered. 'Of course not! I'll hand them over to our Russian friends along with you.' He glanced down at the boat which was now almost alongside the pier. One of the men was hefting a coiled rope in his hands. The other was attaching something that looked suspiciously like a hand grenade to his belt. 'I'm sure they'll have no trouble taking care of a bunch of nosy kids.' He flashed a malevolent look at Drift. 'And I bet they just *adore* vicious little mutts!'

Jack felt his insides turn to water. Suddenly the firing squad didn't seem such a bad idea.

'Just one last thing before we say our goodbyes,' Rudge told Pym. 'I need to see that hand to confirm that you really are Leonard Makepiece.'

Pym slowly removed his right hand from his pocket and held it up.

Three fingers were missing.

'Excellent,' Rudge said. 'The result of sniper fire while on an undercover operation in Serbia, I understand? Now let's invite our friends to join the party.' Still keeping the gun trained on Pym, he sidestepped to the edge of the pier and gave a thumbs-up to the men on the boat.

Suddenly another voice rang out into the night.

'Jack? What are you *doing* out there?'

Everyone looked up to see a blonde girl picking her way along the pier, tugging on a butterfly-patterned umbrella which was turning inside-out in the wind.

Nineteen

Dangerous!

'It's dangerous on the pier!' Josie yelled.

You can say that again, Jack thought grimly. *I've got a madman waving a loaded gun in my face and a boatload of Russian hitmen with AK-47s strapped to their backs waiting to feed me to the fishes. "Dangerous" doesn't even come close!*

Rudge shouted at Josie. 'You! Over here and stand with the others!'

Josie laughed. 'What if I don't want to?' She obviously hadn't noticed the minor detail of the weapon pointing in her direction.

'Do as he says,' Jack shouted. 'He's got a gun!'

'Just move it!' Rudge yelled. He turned and took a step towards Josie.

Suddenly he disappeared.

Or at least, his legs and body disappeared. His head and shoulders were still poking up from a hole in the rotten decking.

The gun had dropped from Rudge's hand and was now lying on a narrow board balanced across the edge of the gaping hole like a gangplank. Rudge reached out for it. But Scott had seen his chance. He sprinted towards the gun, ready to pounce and snatch it away from Rudge.

There was a terrible splintering and cracking noise as more boards began caving in around the hole.

'Stop!' Emily cried.

Scott froze in mid-stride. The decking was shattering around him like thin ice on a pond.

Jack couldn't believe it. He was usually the one leaping headlong into danger! His eyes darted from Scott to Rudge and then to the gun. Rudge's outstretched fingers were almost brushing against the metal. One more second and he'd be able to squeeze the trigger and fire at Scott – who was paralyzed as if by a magic spell only an arm's length away.

'Use this!' Jack looked up just in time to see Josie throwing her umbrella to him. He caught it and pulled the handle out to its full length. Lying flat on his stomach, as close to the hole as he dared, he reached out. If he could just use the umbrella's curved handle to hook the gun and pull it back then Rudge would be the one putting his hands on his head!

Jack had the handle looped over the gun now, but easing it back without knocking it off the edge of the plank required patience and precision – not exactly Jack's strongest traits. He almost had it . . . Behind him he heard Emily snap off a length of metal railing and hold it out to Scott.

'Grab hold of the end!' she was shouting.

Jack reached for the gun. It was almost in his hand now . . .

Suddenly Rudge made a desperate lunge for it. The gun fell off the plank and plummeted into the water far below.

'Blast!' Jack cursed. But at least it meant Rudge couldn't get the gun either. Behind him he heard Emily pull Scott away from the hole to safety. 'Jack, come back!' they were both shouting now. *Don't worry,* he thought. *I'm not hanging around here any longer. These planks are getting wobblier by the second.* But as he was about to shuffle backwards he suddenly he felt a tug on the umbrella. Rudge had grabbed the handle and was trying to pull himself out of the hole. Jack pulled back. He felt the wood beneath him begin to crumble away.

'Let go!' Josie, Emily and Scott all yelled.

Jack let go.

Rudge disappeared through the hole still clutching the butterfly umbrella in his hand. There was a long scream of terror and then a deep booming splash.

Jack felt himself slipping after him. He closed his eyes. This was it! He was plunging headfirst into the abyss. He was about to be sucked down into dark raging waters bristling with submerged wreckage. But at the last moment a pair of hands gripped each of his ankles. He was dragged away from the hole. He sat up to find Emily and Scott kneeling over him. Drift licked his nose. He was alive!

'Cheers, guys!' Jack tried to keep the panic out of his voice. 'I didn't really fancy a swim just now.'

His words were drowned out by a heart-stopping crash. A vast section of the decking had given way around the hole and was sliding into the waves. Jack stared at the chasm that had opened up across the full width of the boardwalk. They were stranded on a tiny rickety island on stilts with no way back to the main pier.

Only Josie remained on the landward side of the rift.

'Stay there,' she yelled. 'I'll call the coastguard.' She turned and ran back along the pier.

Emily heard a man's voice and spun round. She'd forgotten all about Pym! He was leaning against the last remaining section of railing, talking on his mobile phone. Fury rose hot and bitter in Emily's throat. You could take the cool and calm act too far! Hadn't he *noticed* things were getting dicey? What with the violent storm and the collapsing pier and the gun-toting Russians, even Emily wasn't sure how they were going to get out of this alive.

And things were about to get even worse. A grappling hook clattered over the edge of the pier, directly behind Pym, followed by the face and arms of a man in a black waterproof. He was aiming something at Pym . . .

Scott had seen it too. 'Look out!' he yelled at Pym.

But it was too late.

Pym folded to his knees and keeled over. His phone flew out of his hand and scooted along the decking.

Scott dived and caught it millimetres before it shot off the edge of the pier.

'They've killed him!' Jack screamed.

Scott ran to Pym's side. 'No, he's breathing. It must have been one of those tranquilizer darts.'

'Phone . . . ' Pym gasped urgently, trying to lift his head. Scott leaned closer to catch the faint words. 'Helicopter . . . speak to Agent Dynamo . . . rescue . . .' His words tailed off as he lost consciousness.

Scott held Pym's phone to his ear and heard a woman's voice saying 'Hello, hello. Enigma, are you there? Please complete your situation report.'

Scott held the phone away and looked at it in disbelief. That sounded just like . . .

'Aunt Kate?'

'Scott! Is that you?' It *was* Aunt Kate! 'Now listen to me,' she instructed. 'Stand by for airlift. Please confirm your location.'

'End of the old pier on Westward Beach,' Scott replied.

Emily was straining to hear the conversation when Jack pulled her towards him.

The man who'd shot Pym was climbing up over the edge of the pier. Drift charged at him, snarling and growling. The man lost his grip and fell backwards into the waves. Jack cheered, but Emily looked over the side. There were already more grappling hooks, more ropes and at least four more men climbing towards them.

It seemed all hope was lost, but suddenly Jack was pointing up into the sky. 'Look, there's a helicopter!'

Emily heard the whir of blades. Could it be true? Were they really going to be rescued? But who would be crazy enough to fly in a storm like this? There could be a lightning strike any moment!

'Must be the coastguard,' Jack shouted. 'Wow! Josie worked fast!'

'I don't think it was Josie,' Emily yelled back. The helicopter was now close enough for them to see that it didn't have the white and orange paintwork of a coastguard vehicle. It was black and grey, as if designed for stealth. It was circling above them, being tossed back and forth by the wind.

'Aunt Kate sent them!' Scott shouted. 'They're going to airlift us out.' His words were lost in the deafening *chop-chop-chop* of the helicopter blades.

A powerful searchlight suddenly lit up the scene.

Jack, Emily, Scott and Drift huddled together. The downdraft from the helicopter felt like the eye of a tornado. A mighty wave crashed over the end of the pier drenching them all. There was a cry and a splash as another of the Russians fell from his rope.

Seconds later a rescuer was being winched down on a rope from the helicopter. He quickly bundled the comatose Pym into a stretcher harness. 'Be back in a moment. Hang on!' the winchman yelled as he was hoisted away.

Emily was the next to go. She refused to leave without Drift. Somehow the winchman stuffed him inside Emily's harness and secured him with extra straps.

Soon the winch rope was back. Scott strapped Jack into the harness before he could argue. Swinging out over the waves Jack's stomach went into freefall. This was like bungee jumping and the Obliterator ride at Planet Adventure all rolled into one. It'd be fun if it weren't for the crackling of machine-gun fire below him.

And I thought this was going to be a boring evening, Jack thought, as he was being manhandled into the helicopter, where Emily sat with a foil blanket round her shoulders, clinging to Drift.

The winchman was already descending once again.

'We can't risk staying any longer.' The worried voice came from the pilot. 'There's lightning coming!'

Jack felt sick with fear. Yes, Scott was the world's most annoying older brother, but he'd jump out of the helicopter before going without him. 'We can't leave Scott behind!' he cried.

'It's OK,' Emily shouted. 'Look!' She pointed down at the pier.

The winchman was dangling close to Scott. But just as he was about to land on the pier the helicopter banked sharply. The rope was swinging away again.

Scott jumped.

Jack closed his eyes.

When he opened them again he saw the winchman still hanging on the rope below – and Scott was with him!

Scott's feet had hardly left the ground when the end of the pier lurched and collapsed into the sea like the sinking *Titanic*. As the helicopter turned back for the mainland, thunder began to rumble and lightning flashed across the waves.

Twenty

International Espionage

'Wow! So Aunt Kate's a *secret agent*!' Jack whistled. Scott nodded. 'Agent Dynamo.' He'd always suspected there was more to Aunt Kate than met the eye. For an old lady who was into baking and gardening and romantic novels, she'd always seemed to know an awful lot about data encryption and code breaking. Now he knew she hadn't just got it all out of those Dirk Hazard spy blockbusters she loved so much.

'At least there's *one* spy on the island!' Emily laughed.

'Not a *spy*,' Aunt Kate said with a smile, returning to the living room with a tray of drinks and chocolate chip cookies. 'Many years ago I worked in communications for the intelligence service supporting our agents out in the field.'

'So you didn't go on any proper missions?' Jack couldn't hide his disappointment. Having a real spy for a great-aunt would've been so cool!

Aunt Kate smiled again. 'I *may* have been asked to assist with some special covert operations now and then.' She shook her head as Scott, Jack and Emily all began to fire questions at her. 'Sorry, I can't tell you any more. It's a matter of . . .'

' . . . national security!' the friends chorused.

Scott reached for a cookie. He flinched. After last night's dramatic escape from the pier he ached in places he hadn't even known he had. They'd been halfway back to the mainland before the winch line was hoisted all the way up and he was bundled inside the helicopter. Clinging onto the harness had taken every shred of strength in his body. They'd landed at a secret military base somewhere on the mainland, where they'd all been checked over by a team of medics before being driven home.

'Why were you codenamed Dynamo?' Emily asked.

Aunt Kate laughed. 'They called me that because I was always on the go. Between shifts I used to bake cakes and biscuits to take in to keep everyone's energy up.'

Jack helped himself to another cookie, still warm from the oven. It seemed some things about Aunt Kate hadn't changed over the years.

'And you knew Edward Pym in those days?' Scott asked. 'That's when that photo was taken?'

Aunt Kate nodded. 'His real name is Leonard Makepiece. Codename Enigma. One of our finest agents.'

'Were you madly in love?' Jack just couldn't resist asking.

'Maybe you should be the one writing the romantic novels,' Aunt Kate laughed. 'Let's just say we always got on well. So when MI6 contacted me to say he was being relocated to Castle Key I was pleased to be able to meet up with him again.'

'MI6?' Scott asked. 'Not MI5?'

Aunt Kate nodded. 'That's right. MI6 is the overseas intelligence service. MI5 is concerned with internal security.'

'Is Pym still a spy?' Jack asked.

Aunt Kate smiled. 'He's retired from active duty, but still involved in some intelligence gathering work.'

'I'm really sorry,' Emily said dejectedly. 'We thought he was a Russian agent.' Pym – who was just starting to come round when the helicopter landed – had been hurriedly bundled off to another area of the base last night. It was obvious he wasn't coming back to Castle Key.

Aunt Kate shook her head. 'It's not your fault. That man calling himself Rudge had rumbled him already. Leonard will be given another identity and set up in a new location.'

'But why was Rudge—' Scott's question was cut off by the ring of the doorbell.

'Ah, perfect timing,' Aunt Kate said as she got up. 'MI6 said they'd send someone to debrief you. They'll be able to answer that question.'

Emily looked at Scott and Jack, her eyes wide with excitement. A *debriefing* with a real MI6 agent! Maybe Operation Skylark wasn't going to be a total disaster after all!

'This is Olivia Green,' Aunt Kate said as she came back with a smartly dressed young woman in a white shirt and dark grey suit. Her black hair was swept up in a stylish French plait and she wore a tiny communications earpiece. She smiled and shook hands all round. Then she sat on the sofa, placing a smart leather laptop case on the table.

Scott nudged Jack and they exchanged grins. Emily had hero-worshipped Rudge (before they'd found out he was a total fraud, of course) but now she was even *more* star-struck! She clearly wanted nothing more in the world than to *be* Olivia Green!

'What can you tell us about Rudge?' Scott asked.

Olivia Green put down the cup of tea Aunt Kate had handed her. 'Real name Mike Slater. We've had him on our radar for a while so we're very pleased to have finally tracked him down. We've got him in custody now. Your friend Josie called the coastguard and they picked him up from the sea near the pier, clinging to a bit of wreckage. He's battered and bruised but still in one piece.'

'Is he a spy too?' Jack asked.

'No, he's a computer hacker who specializes in making money out of breaking into high-security systems,' Olivia explained. 'He heard on some shady chat site that there was a price on Enigma's head, so he set about finding him to claim the bounty. He wrote some very clever spy software and managed to download it onto Enigma's personal computer over the internet. That's how he traced him to Castle Key. It's such a devious program that none of the existing virus checkers can pick it up. The only loophole turned out to be that Mike Slater accidentally programmed his software to use the same client address port as the one used by the new version of the *Total Strategy* game – so they couldn't run at the same time.'

'Which Enigma never noticed because he didn't have *Total Strategy* on his laptop,' Emily chipped in.

Olivia smiled. 'Exactly. Who knows how many other

people's computers Mike Slater has infected with that virus? Thanks to Scott's detective work we now know which network address the spyware uses and we can shut it down.'

Scott beamed with pride.

'We should've known old Rudge was a hacker,' Jack said. 'He was so pale and scrawny. Must have been from spending hours hunched over his computer. But who was offering a reward for Enigma? Was it this Viktor Kozlov guy that Rudge was going on about?'

'That's right,' Olivia said. 'Kozlov is a millionaire Russian businessman. A few years ago we picked up intelligence that he was supplying weapons to several terrorist groups that were planning to strike important targets in the UK. Enigma was sent in on an undercover operation to find out what was going on, but his cover was blown by a double agent. We managed to disrupt the supplies to the terrorists and get Enigma out of there, but Kozlov made it known through his underworld connections that he wanted revenge. He offered a bounty of a million dollars to anyone who delivered Enigma to him alive.'

'Wow!' Jack breathed. '*Real* spying like in the movies!'

Emily interrupted with another question. The word *delivered* had reminded her of the note she'd translated from Polish. At last she could find out what *Two chimney pots will be delivered on Friday* meant. Olivia

Green was bound to know! Today was Friday so they might be just in time . . .

But Olivia shook her head. 'It wasn't code. The builders were just waiting for a delivery of new Victorian-style chimney pots for the roof at Sunset Lodge.'

'So they really were just ordinary builders?' Scott asked. 'Not bodyguards?'

Olivia took a sip of her tea. 'Not *ordinary* exactly. They're a crew of expert Polish builders we often use for construction projects. They're sworn to secrecy about what they work on. They don't arouse suspicion because local residents just assume that they don't speak English. Enigma was fluent in many languages so he liked to talk to the builders in Polish.'

Emily had never felt so crushed. 'So the note doesn't tell us anything at all?'

Olivia smiled warmly at her. 'On the contrary. It tells me a great deal.'

'What?' Emily asked.

'Do you speak Polish?'

'No,' Emily replied, puzzled by the question. 'Only Spanish because my mum is from Spain.'

Olivia nodded. 'So, you figured out the note was in Polish. That tells me you have great perseverance. Not only that, you were observant enough to see Enigma leave the note in the first place *and* get a photo of it without being spotted. These are qualities we are always looking for in the intelligence services. I'm sure MI6 would love to hear from you as soon as you're old enough. I will be happy to provide you with a reference . . .'

Emily's heart leaped straight from misery to bliss without stopping on the way. *I'm sure MI6 would love to hear from you* . . . It was her dream come true! She hugged Drift who was curled up next to her. She was sure MI6 would be interested in him too!

'Hang on a minute,' Jack said suddenly. 'Those builders weren't *all* Polish. The one with the Welsh accent and the ponytail – he and Pym, sorry, Enigma, were speaking English when they were chasing us round the house.'

Olivia Green smiled. 'Yes, well spotted. Agent Fox is one of ours. He was there to help protect Enigma.' She glanced apologetically at Aunt Kate. 'I'm afraid Enigma has got a bit sloppy with his security since retiring from active service. He should never have gone to that picnic meeting completely unarmed and without Fox – even if he did think it was a *social* appointment.' Olivia smiled at Jack. 'I heard you were the one who figured out that Mr Rudge was making up the codenames as he went along. Well done. You clearly have a knack for . . .'

'Total genius?' Jack suggested, as Olivia paused to think of the right word. 'Sheer brilliance?'

She laughed. 'I was going to say *thinking outside*

the box!' She stood up to leave. 'Must get back to HQ now.' She turned back to the sofa and held up a book. 'Oh, what's this I've been sitting on?' She read the title. '*Extreme Butterflies.* Who's the lepidopterist around here?'

Scott pointed at Jack.

'Hey, me too!' Olivia enthused. 'I got into it on a training mission in New Guinea a few years back.'

'Cool! Did you see a Queen Alexandra Birdwing?' Jack asked, before he could help himself.

Olivia looked impressed. 'Yeah, they were awesome! I love anything to do with nature, don't you?'

Jack didn't like to mention that he'd actually been officially at war with nature for some time. 'Yeah, it's great!' he mumbled.

Suddenly Jack was reminded of Josie. She'd played a big part in saving them from total annihilation on the pier. If she hadn't turned up and distracted Rudge he might not have fallen through the rotten planks. And if she hadn't thrown Jack her butterfly umbrella to knock the gun out of Rudge's reach, events could have turned out very differently. He cleared his throat and turned to Olivia. 'Er, you don't still have any contacts in New Guinea, do you? It's just that I have a friend who really wants to go there on a butterfly safari . . .'

'You mean Josie Morgan?' Olivia asked.

Jack blushed. He should have realized that an MI6

agent would have done background checks on everyone connected with the case.

Olivia smiled. 'Sure. I can put her in touch with a butterfly conservation charity I know. They always want volunteers and they can help with travel costs.'

Jack grinned. He couldn't wait to tell Butterfly Girl the good news!

'And I'd like to invite all three of you to come to MI6 HQ in London for a special personal tour,' Olivia finished.

Emily looked as if she would burst with happiness.

—

'There's just one thing I don't get about all this,' Scott said quietly, after Aunt Kate had left to see Olivia Green to the door. 'If Aunt Kate has nothing to do with the secret service any more, how come she was able to call in that helicopter like that? And how come Pym was still calling her Agent Dynamo?'

'Very mysterious!' Emily agreed. 'Maybe there's still one spy left on the island after all.'

'Which reminds me,' Jack told her, 'you owe me a million pounds.'

Emily laughed. 'No way!'

Jack nodded. 'Oh, yes! You bet me a million pounds that Rudge was an MI5 agent. You lose!' He held out his hand, as if expecting the cash to appear.

Scott grinned at Jack. 'Actually, if we're calling in the bets, I seem to remember *you* saying you'd kiss Mrs Loveday if Pym wasn't a Russian spy!'

Emily laughed. 'This I have to see.' She looked at her watch. 'Mrs L will be at Dotty's now. Let's go!' She puckered her lips at Jack and made for the door.

Jack squirmed in his seat. 'Yeah, well, obviously I didn't mean it!' He laughed and aimed a cushion at Emily. 'OK, it's quits. All bets are off.'

Emily threw the cushion back at him. She missed and hit Scott, who fired two cushions back at her.

Drift leaped up and bounded around barking happily. He loved cushion fights!

When she collapsed onto the sofa a few moments later, Emily heard voices at the front door. Aunt Kate returned to the living room carrying a large basket.

Drift sniffed the air and flicked his ears to Full Alert.

'What's that?' Jack asked. 'You're not planning *another* champagne and strawberry picnic, are you?'

Aunt Kate laughed and shook her head. 'Before he left, Edward asked me one last favour. He wants me to look after his cat. One of the builders just delivered him.' She placed the basket on the ground and looked hesitantly at Emily. 'Maybe you could take Drift out into the garden while I settle Boomerang in?'

As they played fetch-the-stick and tag with Drift on the lawn and then watched him chase a squirrel up the chestnut tree, Scott, Jack and Emily discussed the situation in dismay. Boomerang was a cute little guy, but if he moved in with Aunt Kate, what about poor Drift? Those two clearly couldn't be in the same room together without World War Three breaking out! They couldn't deny poor little Boomerang a home, but would that mean that Drift would be banished from Stone Cottage for ever?

Emily looked round to give Drift a consoling hug, but he was nowhere to be seen.

'Uh oh!' Jack groaned. 'He must have gone inside and started chasing Boomerang already!' They all hurried back into the cottage – expecting to find a terrified tabby clawing its way up the curtains while Drift gnashed his teeth below. But to their surprise they found Aunt Kate sitting calmly on the sofa. She smiled and put her finger to her lips. Then she pointed towards the hearth rug.

Drift and Boomerang were curled up together.

Boomerang sighed in his sleep. Drift licked the top of the little cat's head head.

Scott grinned at Jack and Emily. 'Looks like the start of a beautiful friendship!' He knelt and stroked Boomerang's soft fur. He'd always wanted a cat.

Jack flopped down on the rug next to him. 'So, what shall we do tomorrow?'

'I know!' Scott joked. 'Let's go birdwatching. I'll bring the Digestives!'

'Or we could go butterfly spotting?' Emily laughed, tickling Drift's ears.

Jack groaned. 'No, thanks! It's too dangerous!' Then he laughed. 'How about a spot of international espionage instead?'

After all, in Castle Key, *anything* was possible!

Collect all the Adventure Island *books . . .*

OUT NOW!